**Longarm figured there was only
one gunslick tracking him
through the moonlit sage. . . .**

He learned he was wrong when a hoarse voice screamed, "Harry! Behind you!" The next few split seconds proceeded to get noisy as hell.

Longarm fired at the one he could see. The cuss went down. Damn! Which one had it been?

He worried less about who he might have shot when the night was rent by a fusillade of repeater rounds pegged in his general direction.

It was downright stupid in a night action to stay in one place as you fired blind. Longarm landed on one side as he threw himself in the dirt. He just kept rolling and rolling till he came up in a spread-leg crouch.

It only took one bullet to silence the crackle of gunfire in the distance.

TABOR EVANS

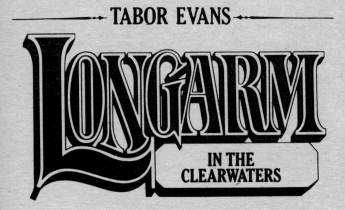

LONGARM

IN THE
CLEARWATERS

JOVE BOOKS, NEW YORK

LONGARM IN THE CLEARWATERS

A Jove Book / published by arrangement with
the author

PRINTING HISTORY
Jove edition / November 1989

ISBN: 0-515-10173-7

Jove Books are published by The Berkley Publishing Group,
200 Madison Avenue, New York, New York 10016.
The name ''JOVE'' and the ''J'' logo
are trademarks belonging to Jove Publications, Inc.

PRINTED IN THE UNITED STATES OF AMERICA

10 9 8 7 6 5 4 3 2 1

Chapter 1

Longarm and his boss, U.S. Marshal William Vail of the Denver District Court, were about as different as any two lawmen could have been without one or the other resorting to crime.

The tall, tanned Longarm thought best on the move and preferred digging postholes to paperwork, while the older and squattier Billy Vail hunted more like a slick old spider, hardly ever moving from the center of his web of interoffice communications as he read and reread letters and wires from other lawmen, coast to coast, in a manner that reminded Longarm of a crackpot stamp collector searching through his albums for something that had likely never been there to begin with.

Vail was almost convinced that Longarm was an impetuous youth who sort of stumbled over wanted outlaws in the process of tracking down wine, women and three-for-a-nickel cheroots. But the two of them hunting the same want, each in his own way, made an almost unbeatable combination.

By way of example, take the time Longarm forked himself aboard the wrong pony one evening, over near Lookout Mountain. It made him feel dumb as soon as he saw he'd done so, but in truth it was a natural enough mistake, once you studied on it.

Longarm had ridden out from Denver aboard a buckskin gelding, borrowed from his pals at the Diamond K on the edge of town, to compare notes with the local county law on a recent rash of robberies in and about the mining community of Golden. He'd just as naturally saddled the borrowed bronc with the McClellan he could afford to keep in his hired corner room on the unfashionable side of Cherry Creek. So when he tethered all the results in front of the Golden City Hall, it was with the distinct impression he'd dismounted from a McClellan saddle carried by a run-of-the-mill albeit light-complexioned cow pony. It was close to sunset, and feeling no call at the moment to take notes on the six or eight other mounts tethered along the same public hitching rail, Longarm didn't. He just went inside, jawed for a spell with the old cuss holding down the night desk and then, as they both agreed the local stickups had been annoying as hell but hardly federal offenses, they shook on it and Longarm went back out front to mount up some more for the roughly fifteen-mile ride back to Denver.

More annoyed at the thought of the tedious waste of his own time than concerned about the way his mount might feel about it, Longarm had untethered the buckskin with the McClellan saddle, or at any rate *some* buckskin with a McClellan saddle, and forked himself aboard before it came to him that something seemed sort of out of joint up here this evening. He knew his own saddle a heap better than he could have been expected to know a borrowed cow pony. Longarm's McClellan had been designed by the one and original General George McClellan of wartime notoriety, the ungainly looking but pragmatic army saddle serving to bolster Longarm's opinion that no man was all fool or all wise. For if poor old George had botched the Peninsular Campaign and led the Union Army into the mutual bloodbath of Antietam, he'd sure known his oats when it came to military gear, and old U. S. Grant had inherited an army equipped second to none.

But this particular McClellan saddle felt out of sorts

between Longarm's legs, as if the tree might be cracked, and he was used to riding with his stirrup leathers longer. So he reined in, out in the middle of the now-dark street, and dismounted to take a stroll around the disconcerting pony, which turned out to be a mare with an unfamiliar brand, for openers.

Longarm chuckled sheepishly and murmured, "Sorry, ma'am. In the soft light of gloaming I took you for another critter entire." But then, as he led her afoot back to the hitching rail, he had to add, "So where in blue blazes is the damned Diamond K gelding that's supposed to be some damned where around here?"

It was a simple question with a simple enough answer as soon as you studied on it. Some other cuss had made the same dumb mistake in the tricky light. It could only be a question of time before he, too, noticed he was riding the wrong mount to Lord only knew where and naturally turned back, the same way, to put things to right. Meanwhile, there was just no way Longarm could head back to Denver on another man's mount, horse theft being punishable by death under the draconian stock and mining laws of Colorado. But at the same damned time there wasn't a saloon or even a chili parlor in sight, and there was no telling when the other rider might see the error of his ways and get his fool ass and that Diamond K buckskin back here.

Longarm held the reins in one hand and fished out a cheroot with the other as he stared about in the gathering gloom of Golden, muttering to the apparently indifferent mare, "I know you don't drink Maryland rye, but you could likely use some branch water, and there's that tap-room across from the municipal corral. So that's where I reckon we'd best wait for your rider and my righteous mount."

Suiting actions to words he lit the smoke and remounted to ride the short distance, knowing the public corral served

3

as a sort of pond for stray horseflesh in addition to its other functions. But things didn't work out quite that way.

For just as Longarm swung the mysterious mare around to ride off a modest ways, the buckskin he'd borrowed at the Diamond K loped out of the darkness at him, well lathered and packing what seemed a raving lunatic with a gun. The outraged stranger's aim was fortunately as wild as his intentions. But after Longarm had rolled from the saddle to get out of the way of the first wild shots, he felt obliged to firmly state, covered behind the strange buckskin from the strange rider's fire, "That's enough, goddamn it! You peg one more shot my way and I mean to return your fire, you total asshole!"

The strange rider blew Longarm's low-crowned tobacco-brown Stetson off by way of reply. So Longarm fired back, over the saddlebags he didn't recall being behind the cantle of his own saddle, and the saddle he'd started out with that afternoon was suddenly empty.

As the borrowed Diamond K gelding ran off a ways, Longarm held on to the reins of the other buckskin and hauled her toward her more proper but downed rider, whether she liked the scent of blood and gunsmoke or not. By this time doors were popping open all up and down the street and folk were coming out like clockwork cuckoos. A familiar voice coming from the side door of the city hall just up the way demanded some explaining. So Longarm called back, "I'm still working on it," and hunkered near the sprawled figure of the gent he'd just had to shoot in simple self-defense. "Evening, pard. As I was trying to explain just now, we swapped ponies, innocent, by mutual mistake. Where did I hit you, old son?"

At closer range, the trigger-happy cuss who'd brought such misfortune on his fool self turned out to be a youth in his late teens or early twenties. He was dressed top hand in broken-in denims but spanking-new boots with silver-mounted Mex spurs that matched his fancy buscadero gun

4

rig. The Texas hat upside down in the dust near his bear-greased head was as new and white as the belly feathers of a Peking duck. His eyes were open but staring up at Longarm sort of glassy. Longarm reholstered his cross-drawn .44-40 and thumbnailed a match alight. He was moving it back and forth above the stranger's staring eyes when the older lawman in charge of the Golden night shift joined him to whistle softly and opine, "That boy looks about done for, Deputy Long!"

Longarm shook out the match, muttering, "There's no doubt about it. I surely wish there was a way to stop an armed and dangerous man in poor light without hurting him, but as there just ain't, I just now killed the poor dumb brute. You'd know better than me how his home spread is apt to take his sudden demise, pard."

But the local lawman answered, "No I wouldn't. He ain't off any spread in these parts, unless they just now hired him for the fall roundup."

Longarm shook his head and replied, "Too early in the summer for anyone to be taking on extra trail hands. On the other hand, he's outfitted sort of prima donna, and most outfits can use a real top hand, most any time, with the price of beef so high this season. We'd best pat him down for some I.D. That has to have just guessing beat."

But despite the self-indulgent trimmings of the hot-tempered young cuss and the seventy-odd dollars in paper and specie he packed loose in his jeans, he didn't have so much as a wallet on him, let alone one scrap of personal identification. As Longarm was morosely remarking on this, the other lawman was going through the dead rider's saddlebags aboard the buckskin mare. Longarm struck another match in hopes of finding the mysterious stranger's pistol before anyone in the crowd drifting in could steal it. He'd just spotted the nickel-plated Starr .36 when the older gent pawing through the possibles strapped to the mare's McClellan whistled loudly and said, "I can see now how come he got so vexed at you for riding off on this other critter this evening!''

Longarm scooped up the flashy six-gun to join the old-timer on the far side as the latter struck a light of his own. Longarm stared soberly into the chest-high saddlebag by matchlight and whistled some himself as he saw it was almost filled with paper money. A *lot* of paper money. The older county lawman told Longarm, ''Whether this young rascal was offending federal or not, he sure as death and taxes never made this money punching cows!''

That would have been about the end of it, under the jurisdiction of anyone less spidery than Marshal Billy Vail. For to no great surprise at all, nobody saw fit to come forward and claim the body, or the money and tolerable pony that went with it. Folk along the Front Range who'd been robbed in recent memory naturally stopped by for a look-see as the dead youth lay on cracked ice and rock salt in the Golden Morgue for as long as anyone could stand it. But while some recalled a member of the outlaw trio they'd been held up by as a masked man on a buckskin, mounts of that coloration were not all that rare, and there was just no saying what a face under a feed-sack mask might or might not have looked like in life.

In death it was commencing to turn all sorts of funny colors and so, after taking a couple of photographs for future reference, the county coroner ordered the stinky son of a bitch out of his morgue and into the 'dobe soil of the potter's field out back of the boys' reform school. Longarm agreed it would do the young prisoners good to pick and shovel six feet down in summer-baked dirt with the pine box stewing on the dry grass nearby. For the gun waddie they were planting couldn't have been all that much older than the reform school kids, and Longarm couldn't help wondering whether a less-fatal introduction to death might not have done the hasty tempered young cuss some good. It was a lot easier to become a self-taught gunslick shooting at bottles and such that neither shot back nor bled and shit their pants when a bullet tore through them. Longarm had been a tad younger than the youth he'd just been forced to kill when he'd been forced to kill for the first time at a place called Shiloh. He hadn't enjoyed the experience. He'd been told by older and wiser gunfighters, until he'd gotten to be an older and wiser gunfighter in his own right, that he owed his protracted existence to a certain distaste for killing or even fighting, tempered by his matter-of-fact acceptance that there were times it couldn't be avoided, and that winning had losing beat by miles.

The hotheads and cruel-streaked cusses who *enjoyed* the tang of trouble and went looking for it seldom lasted long enough to get good at gunfighting. But they tended to put nicer folk on the ground along their own way to the grave. So Longarm's conscience didn't bother him, once it was obvious he'd taken out a bad man of one variety or another. So he wasn't even thinking about the incident over Golden way the morning he showed up on time for work, it being payday at the downtown Denver Federal Building.

Young Henry, the prissy looking but fairly tough law clerk who played the typewriter for Billy Vail, blinked in surprise at the unexpected sight of Longarm in the office before ten, but he recovered to say, "The paymaster just sent word he won't be by this side of noon. But the boss assumed you might not know this and so he told me to send you right on back to see him when you got here, you eternal optimist."

Longarm winced and said, "A man has to be optimistic, riding for the Justice Department. Lord knows they don't pay us enough to last all the way to the next payday, unless we dream some."

Henry just sniffed and made some dry remark about gents who thought they could manage every known vice on a senior deputy's pay. Longarm resisted the temptation to suggest old Henry might be at least a couple of perversions up on him, knowing it might not be fair to the weak-jawed simp, and ambled in to the inner sanctum of the more ferocious-looking Billy Vail.

When Vail shot a thoughtful glance at the banjo clock on one oak-paneled wall, Longarm said, "Henry told me. You're going to have to advance me some eating money if you don't want me abusing myself and the free lunch at the Parthenon Saloon on Uncle Sam's time, orders or no orders."

Vail growled, "You won't be at the Parthenon or any other such place in Denver, come noon. Didn't my fool clerk tell you I've already signed you a twelve-hundred-mile travel voucher you can cash good as gold?"

Longarm sank down into the leather guest chair across the cluttered desk from Vail's swivel-chaired as well as fat behind, saying, "Henry's had it in for me ever since I aced him out with that bubbly blonde in the land management office down the hall. If we're talking six hundred miles going and coming back, alone, we're talking seventy-odd sweet smackers. If I'm supposed to come back with a prisoner, at twelve cents a mile instead of six, I like your notion even better, boss."

Vail smiled thinly and replied, "I assumed you might. But I ain't sending you up to the Clearwater country just to near double your pay for August. Do you recall that cuss you shot over to Golden a week or more back?"

Longarm nodded, reaching absently under his tobacco-tweed frock coat for a cheroot as he replied, "I do. But what might his unruly behavior in Colorado have had to do with Idaho Territory, let alone parts of the same that have never been properly mapped, or even settled enough to stick up?"

Vail got out a more expensive albeit more pungent cigar as if to defend himself, growling, "Just shut up and listen, and watch where you flick them damned ashes, and I'll tell

8

you a tale of slick detection that makes up for your care-free ways with that .44-40.''

Vail waited until they'd both lit up before he leaned back expansively and explained, ''The Treasury Department in its infinite wisdom prints different numbers on each and every silver certificate it issues. Since all post offices and many banks keep track of at least larger bills, I now feel free to inform you that some of the money that young cuss was packing in his saddlebags was hotter than a whore's pillow on a Saturday night with the herds in town.''

''The boys over in Golden allowed about as much,'' Longarm said. ''A more honest gent might not have gotten near as wild eyed about a small fortune he could just plain reclaim as his own lawful property. But what might stick-ups on the Front Range have to do with the Clearwater country way up north, Billy? To begin with it's on the far side of the Great Divide, as well as just plain far.''

Vail scowled and growled, ''Don't tell me where the infernal thousand square miles of busted-up granite might be, goddamn it. You're all too right about the Clearwater country being one of the biggest patches of virgin wilderness left out our way. Most of it's never been properly surveyed, if explored at all. But there are a few settlements along the Clearwater River, albeit not up-country from whence its many headwaters bust outta the many a granite canyon.''

He rummaged through the papers cluttering the top of his desk, which had all the grace and beauty of a pack rat's nest, found one penciled scrap of yellow foolscap he was looking for, and read it back to himself before saying, rather smugly, ''The dead man's buckskin didn't just *look* cayuse to me. When I checked its odd brand I found out a French-Canadian-Cayuse breed called Gaston or Gus Arquette had recorded said brand with the Idaho chapter of the Cattlemen's Protective Association. It seems Arquette

9

enjoys quite a rep up yonder as a breeder and dealer in sudden horseflesh.''

Longarm blew a thoughtful smoke ring, peered through it at old Vail, and said, ''I never got to race that buckskin mare I mounted by mistake that evening, but I'll take your word she was frisky or even Cayuse bred. But what about it? It's no secret that the Cayuse nation got as famous dealing in horseflesh as some others got dealing with the army. There are cayuse ponies all over the west and likely back Esat, by now.''

Vail nodded soberly but said, ''You mean there are jug-headed paints and buckskins with no breeding papers who just *might* have a streak of true cayuse in 'em. Horse traders like to assure you the scrub stock they're pushing could have some Morgan or Arab ancestry as well. Almost anything on four legs looks something like some real horse.''

Longarm didn't argue. So Vail went on, ''The true cayuse war pony, like them other famous breeds, must come down to more modern times from a sport of nature some early Indian was smart enough to spot and inbreed to type. Most nations know, or once knew something about breeding stock, but nobody but the Cayuse ever did it scientifically as the rest of us. The results, as most whites now know as well as any Indian, was a rawhide and whalebone critter of undistinguished appearance and outstanding speed and endurance.''

Longarm suppressed a yawn and protested, ''Damn it, Billy, you know I rode for many a cow spread before I signed on with Uncle Sam six or eight years ago. That young cuss I shot it out with in Golden favored a Starr revolver and a cayuse pony to get by as a sort of impulsive stickup man. Both his gun and his pony must have come from some damned where. Are you saying this horse-breeding breed up Idaho way reported that buckskin mare being stolen?''

10

Vail shook his bullet head, blowing smoke out both nostrils like a mean bull that had just figured out which wavering blur was the matador's cape and which was the matador's ass, and told Longarm, "He did not. I wired the law up in Orofino, the only town worth mention near Arquette's spread, as soon as we pinned his Double Tipi brand down. They reported back that as far as they've heard all is serene up yonder."

Longarm shrugged and said, "That sounds fair. That young gunslick could have picked up that particular pony almost anywhere or anytime since your mighty slim suspect sold her to begin with. You know outlaws would rather steal a pony or, hell, a new hat, before they'd pay for it. What does that old breed have to say about the bill of sale that might go with that buckskin mare?"

"Arquette doesn't know you're heading his way," Vail answered firmly. "I asked you to just hush and let me explain my own line of reasoning."

So Longarm didn't bother to answer and Vail said, "That's better, and watch them damned ashes! I know as well as you do that it takes more than one robin to make a spring. So I'm not going off half cocked over one restless youth aboard a Clearwater cayuse with his own fat share of some recent robberies along the infernal Front Range. I get reports of such unlawful behavior from all over, and a mighty interesting pattern seems to be emerging from the mists, if only that fool Henry would leave these damned papers on this desk the hell alone!"

Vail gathered a telegram here and a Wanted flier there as he pawed through the mess, muttering, "I keep telling the kid that if I wanted anyone neatening up my desk I'd ask for someone a heap prettier from the stenographer pool down the hall, but I reckon sissies are as bad as women when it comes to fucking things up to make 'em look more tiddle-tidy. I can't find that one report from Fort Smith for shit. But here we go . . ."

11

He fanned his documentation like oversized playing cards as he told Longarm, "It saves time if I just say things in sum. What I got here is a serious rash of armed robberies from Montana Territory to Texas, all involving a trio using much the same mask methods. They favor easy-to-get and easy-to-get-rid-of feed sacks over their heads. They ride in fast, around quitting time, to afford themselves some after-sundown riding by the time a posse can gather to chase after 'em. One always holds all three mounts out front whilst the other two do the out-and-out robbing. More'n one witness who knows which end of a cow pony the shit might fall from has opined all the ponies involved had cayuse lines, and more than one has read that same Double Tipi brand."

Longarm started to flick ashes on the rug, remembered just in time, and rose to flick them in the big copper ashtray on Vail's desk, instead, as he objected, "I fail to see all that many robin birds, Billy. Everyone's agreed that old boy over to Golden had to be part of that three-man team, and he had to riding some damned breed of pony."

"I ain't finished, damn it!" Vail snapped. "We can't be talking about *one* three-man gang riding cayuse ponies. Cayuse can carry a man fast and far on the owlhoot trail, but holding up a post office in Montana on a Monday and a Texas bank on a Tuesday is galloping to ridiculous lengths. When you throw in a payroll robbery over in Arkansas that same Tuesday evening it gets even sillier."

Longarm blew another thoughtful smoke ring, softly whistled through it, and decided, "So we're talking about more than one gang, using the same methods and wearing much the same outfits."

Vail nodded and said, "Same outfits entire, down to identical Starr .36s and buckskin Clearwater cayuse mounts. Add it up."

Longarm did. He said with a scowl, "I don't see how so many outlaws could choose the same brand of shooting

12

iron and even match the colors of their Indian ponies accidental. They, or more likely some slicker mastermind, seem to be out to convince us all we're dealing with one small gang when, in point of fact, I read it as at least nine, operating identical but separate.''

''Me and the Texas Rangers make it more like an even dozen. Neither the feed sacks nor the Starr .36s would be hard to come by in any cow town worth mention, and the outlaws may well get rid of both their masks and holdup weapons between jobs. So it's them buckskin Indian ponies, branded so distinctly, we might be able to backtrack to some point of common ground, see?''

Longarm grimaced and said, ''I see you could be sending me on a snipe hunt, and I see at least one hole in your grand design. Have you lost track of the simple fact that the cuss I shot it out with that night in Golden hadn't thrown his Starr .36 away worth mention, boss?''

Vail shrugged and replied, ''Let's not pick nits. I never said I knew for sure they got rid of their cheap pistols between jobs. I only said it seemed likely to me.''

''It seems likely to me, too. So now you can hush and let *me* add things more interesting.''

Vail did. So Longarm continued, ''I'd have noticed if three gents on Indian ponies or, hell, elephants, had robbed anything or anybody in Golden that evening. But what if just one member of an outlaw trio rode in that evening to scout a potential target? What if he tethered his cayuse to move about afoot? What if I foiled a robbery, accidental, by confusing and losing them one member if not the leader of their team?''

Vail nodded grudgingly, but pointed out, ''Anything's possible. But whatever happened happened more than a week ago. The survivors you never met up with have to be long gone by now, old son.''

Longarm shook his head and asked, ''Where in the code of the common criminal does it read everyone else has to

13

go straight if one member of the gang gets killed or even caught alive, Billy? The pals that one cuss was scouting for know he never told us a thing, assuming they can afford to read the *Denver Post*. He'd have hardly been scouting for anyone if they hadn't had a local stickup in mind. So whatever it was is still waiting to be stuck up, and when the sun begins to set this evening we will be talking about a payday night, won't we?''

Billy Vail started to say something dumb. But he hadn't gotten to boss so many others around by being dumb, so he nodded gravely and said, ''Right, most stock spreads and Uncle Sam pay once a month, but a lot of business establishments in towns pay their help every two weeks.''

Longarm smiled wolfishly and said, ''If they were out to skim the mid-month rewards of someone's honest labor when I threw their timing off, consider how tempting this big bonanza payday has to look to the leftover rascals, now that they've taken time to get replacements for the pony and rider they lost that first time.''

Vail still looked dubious. Longarm insisted, ''You said yourself you suspected some mastermind of sending out teams of not-so-bright riders pretending to be one bunch. He'd hardly go to that much trouble and then just let 'em pick their targets. Am I safe in guessing most of the stickups so far have been for considerable profit instead of mere fun?''

Vail nodded soberly and said, ''Never less than five figures, and each time the getaway was slick as a whistle. I follow your drift about the jobs being well planned and scouted in advance. But after that I sort of lose you. For while Golden ain't all that large, we're not talking a crossroads with a general store and maybe a mailbox worth robbing. How could we even hope to stake out everything worth stealing in a town that size, on such short notice?''

''We've got the rest of the morning and all afternoon to work with, boss,'' Longarm insisted. ''They won't hit less

14

than an hour this side of sundown. So we can forget the banks and figure on a check casher or, hell, any one of the bigger saloons or cathouses over yonder.''

He saw Vail needed more convincing, so he said, ''We don't have to stake out anything in town, direct. Golden is tucked into the foothills of the Front Range, between Castle Rock and Lookout Mountain, so—''

''So there's only so many ways to ride in and out!'' Vail cut in with a nasty grin. ''And any three riders loping out along any infernal trail on matching buckskin ponies ought to be easy enough to spot from atop either of them rises overlooking the whole town. So what are you waiting for, a kiss good-bye? You and the boys got some riding ahead of you, you lazy cuss!''

Chapter 2

The city of Denver, along with the shortgrass and soap weed surrounding it, sits atop thick layers of fine silt and clay washed down from the Rockies, looming just to the west. So while the gold dust in Cherry Creek had long since given out, there was still a heap of clay quarrying going on just west of the city limits, making Denver a serious shipper of pottery and bricks as well as sheep and cattle, dead or alive. So later that same day Longarm waved his small but serious posse of fellow federal deputies off the post road to Golden for a powwow in a wide but shallow clay pit he knew to be recently abandoned.

As he reined in and swung the buckskin cayuse he now had his own saddle aboard to face the other thirteen riders, he called out, "We'd best get a few things straight in our heads before we go on into Golden so impressive. To begin with I don't want us to impress anyone all that much. The trio of desperados we're after may be in town already, waiting for the shadows to stretch out a mite, or they may ride in after us from wherever they've been hiding out between jobs. Either way, we don't want to have to go through all this tedious shit again, so we'd best stake 'em out discreet and nail 'em the first time."

Deputy Flynn, who always reminded Longarm of a baby-faced choirboy prone to secret vices, raised his free hand for attention and demanded, "Ain't you taking a lot for granted, Longarm? How do you know for certain that the two you failed to nail that last time are anywhere in Colorado right now?''

Longarm looked disgusted and replied, ''If I knew where half the crooks in this cruel world might be right now, I wouldn't be here jawing with you other overworked and underpaid bastards. I'd be in Washington, running the damned department. So let's eat the apple a bite at a time, damn it. We plain don't know whether the rascals we're after will show up this evening or not. But if they do show up we don't want 'em to spot us first. So here's the way we'd best position ourselves in and about Golden, once we get there.''

They never got there. Longarm was in the middle of explaining his grand design, involving lone lookouts on both Castle Rock and Lookout Mountain, with the rest of the posse out of sight but ready to ride on lower ground, when Deputy Smiley, sitting tall in the saddle atop a clay mound closer to the post road, called out to Longarm in a curiously soft tone, ''Don't nobody make no noise and don't nobody but Longarm ease over this way. We got us some interesting company coming out from Denver right now.''

Longarm didn't need a second invite. He heeled the buckskin mare up the modest slope to join Smiley, took a gander at the trio of riders moving west from Denver at an easy but mile-eating lope, and muttered, ''Jesus H. Christ!''

For the three strangers fit his picture down to everything but the feed-sack masks they likely had in their saddlebags at the moment. All three wore nondescript blue denim jackets and jeans and all three rode jug-headed buckskin ponies that looked as if they came from the same litter, if only their species gave birth to litters. The clay quarry was close to a quarter mile off the dusty post road, so they were too far off to make out any brands or the breed of their six-guns. Smiley observed quietly, ''If that ain't them, they ought to please the boss just as well. My

18

mama was part Pawnee and I'll bet you her old gray head that all three of them ponies are cayuse!"

Longarm simply replied, "No argument about that, Smiley. But not even Billy Vail can hold anyone more than seventy-two hours on pure suspicion. We'd best let 'em pass on by and see how sudden they ride back from Golden, later. If they've been holed up in the city all this time they'll likely use this very same route to get back there, after they circle some in the soft light of gloaming. Maybe, if we left you, Dutch, and Guilfoyle right about here—"

Then all bets were off as Smiley grunted, "Shit, they've spotted us. They must not like what they see and, Kee-rist, look at them ponies go!"

Longarm didn't have time to answer. For as he saw the three mysterious riders break for the north across rolling but wide-open shortgrass range, he was already heeling his own cayuse after them. Smiley had been right. Any cayuse, including the one he was on, could move like spit on a hot stove and, if a rider failed to pay attention, he could wind up spilt like milk from an overfilled bucket. For neither cowboys nor Indians trained mounts to carry kids to school and back at a prissy pace.

Whether chasing buffalo for an Indian or cattle for a white man with a throw rope, the pony of the western plains was bred to act and think, if not eat, as a beast of prey. Depending on the way it had been trained to hunt, it streaked in to put its rider just to the right of a running buffalo or just to the left of an often faster beef critter. Its rider was supposed to do all the worrying about staying aboard. The pony wasn't trained to give a shit. So many a trained cavalryman as well as many a greenhorn had been left in midair by a quicksilver-gaited high plains pony swerving to avoid a prairie dog hole, a scrap of windblown paper, or its own somewhat wild imagination.

It got worse aboard a pure cayuse, Longarm noticed

almost at once. For this was the first time he'd let the buckskin mare run flat out since first he'd mounted her that time by mistake and, as if to let him know she rated more respect, she tore after her three buckskin cousins in great catlike bounds, sidestepping soap weed Longarm could see and likely horny-toad shit he never noticed at all. He forgave her for her erratic progress across the rolling sea of grass when one of the riders out in front of them twisted in his own saddle to peg a round at Longarm.

He missed by a wide margin, of course. Then yet another of them seemed inspired to open fire on him and Longarm was suddenly aware he was all alone out there.

He knew better than to blame his followers. Nothing they were mounted on could have followed Longarm and the riders he was chasing far enough to matter, at this pace. Longarm had chosen the dead outlaw's cayuse from the federal pond with just such a possible event in mind. So while it felt sort of lonesome, it was no great surprise to Longarm when he topped a rise to see the three riders he was chasing had reined in to dismount and spread out along the next rise north. Longarm didn't look back. He didn't have to. He knew they wouldn't be making a stand, even at three-to-one odds, had there been others on his side in sight.

The three of them seemed out to stop him with six-guns, making them a mite optimistic or desperate, in Longarm's opinion. For he'd naturally come this far with his Winchester attached to his personal McClellan and so, as he rode across the wide shallow draw between them, he naturally drew the carbine instead of his six-gun with his free hand, and this inspired at least one of the gents up ahead to drop his .36 like a hot potato and reach for the clear blue sky above.

But then one of the others with him fired, not at Longarm, but into the left kidney of the would-be quitter. So Longarm reined in, took careful if one-handed aim with his Winchester, and blew the sore loser's hat off, along with a good gob of his stubborn skull.

Levering another round into the chamber of a Winchester, one-handed, was possible but clumsy, even without that one son of a bitch left pegging pistol shots one's way. So Longarm's hat went flying, fortunately without any of his head, and when he did have a damned round lever-jerked into the chamber he missed his own target as well. So he rolled from his saddle to land on his heels and move in afoot, firing right. But then the sneaky son of a bitch had run over the far side of the rise, dragging his own pony with him, and as Longarm grasped his intent and turned to remount his own cayuse, the infernal mare danced away from him, shaking her muzzle to keep the reins out from under her sassy hooves while he cussed and she rolled her big brown eyes like the female pain in the ass she was.

He tried flirting back, holding out one empty fist as if he had at least a sugar cube in it. But he might never have recovered the damn fool critter had not Smiley, Dutch, and Flynn come over the crest to the south at last, inspiring the mare to trot over to Longarm like a big pup who knew it had been naughty.

As he grabbed the reins, recovered his hat, and mentioned the dog-food plant in town, Smiley reined in to ask, "What happened? Did she spill you?"

To which Longarm could only reply in a tone of self-loathing, "I'd say it was sort of mutual. I volunteered to get off and she didn't want me back aboard. Before you ask, I dismounted to shoot it out safer with those rascals we were chasing."

Smiley gazed north at the grassy skyline to remark, "You mean *you* were chasing, don't you? Everything my dear momma's people had to say about Cayuse horse traders and the horses they trade in was the simple truth. So what do we tell Billy Vail, now?"

Longarm swung himself back aboard the wayward buck-skin, slid his Winchester back in its boot, and replied, "We tell 'em one of 'em got away. The other two are up yonder in the grass. Lord only knows where their ponies went. But we'd best start scouting for 'em. I'll be surprised as hell if we find any I.D. on the two down. But they must have kept their matched ponies some damned where in Denver, and whether we locate the one rider that got away or not, I'd sure like to find someone more honest who can give us a line on any brands they were packing on their buckskin hides."

Smiley nodded and said, "If two or more can be shown to be off that Idaho spread, we'll know Billy Vail is on to something, right?"

Longarm grimaced and replied, "I sure as shit don't want to go all the way up yonder on a hunch. For the son of a bitch who just shot my hat off couldn't have ridden half that far, just now."

Longarm had oft remarked that the prisons of the land wouldn't have to be built half so large had not so many crooks suffered delusions of common sense. Most acted as if breaking the law was an even contest between them and the rest of humankind. They didn't seem to notice they were a mite outnumbered. Or that if only one honest man in ten was half as smart as they were, that still added up to an awesome amount of brainpower on the side of the law.

So it hardly mattered, in the end, that the lads out to pull a mighty slick stickup in Golden had made every effort to blend in to working-class society in nearby Denver while they'd planned their derring do. Once Longarm, or to be more precise, Billy Vail and the whole Denver office, suspected just that much, it only took a few short days to prove it.

To begin with Longarm's outfit didn't have to do all the hunting alone. Some schoolboys recovered one of the dead

22

outlaw's ponies grazing sedge along the west bank of the South Platte and, after riding it in turns for a time, thought they'd best turn it over to Denver P.D. Meanwhile the other dead man's buckskin had somehow made it across the shallow but treacherous river in an apparent desire to get back to its stall and some oats, only to be caught by some slightly older boys pushing sheep about in the Denver stockyards. That gave Denver P.D. two matched buckskins wearing the same brand. They didn't have to know for certain what a cayuse pony might or might not look like. They only had to recall that the U.S. marshal over at the Federal Building was looking for uninhabited cow ponies that could be branded Double Tipi and the rest just followed as the night the day.

Meanwhile Deputy Guilfoyle had been canvasing livery stables and hit pay dirt near 19th and Wynkoop, where an otherwise not-too-brilliant Arapaho stable hand recalled curry-combing more than one buckskin branded Double Tipi, now that it had been pointed out to him that he could be wrong about that brand having been meant as a sort of sloppy pair of triangles. Better yet, being himself a High Plains Horse Indian, however calmed down by an Indian Agency boarding school, the Arapaho felt qualified to opine all three buckskins had looked Cayuse-bred to him.

That was the end of the trail as far as Deputy Guilfoyle could follow it. The stable hand admitted all white men looked a lot alike to him. But then Sergeant Nolan of Denver P.D. found a little old Hungarian landlady who hired out her upstairs rooms to railroad or stockyard workers and such. She recalled three nice young gents who'd apparently checked out without seeing fit to tell either her or one other boarder when or why. So Nolan had talked her into a look-see at their baggage without the formality of a search warrant, and while the names Brown, Green, and Black seemed highly unimaginative, a couple of male boarders with strong stomachs were able to identify the two bodies in the Denver Morgue as Green and Black, leaving Brown, Horatio Junior, as the one who got away.

How far he'd flown was of course up for grabs. Longarm opined, and Billy Vail had to agree, that Junior Brown, as they thought of him, was holing up in the depths of downtown Denver rather than streaking for the distant Clearwater country aboard that one still-missing buckskin cayuse. For there was naturally an all-points bulletin out with that in mind, and every law outfit with a Western Union office in the same town was on the prod for such a horse and rider.

With both federal and local lawmen scouting for such an easy to I.D. pony inside the Denver city limits, it soon became just as obvious that the surviving outlaw hadn't picked another public livery stable to board his cayuse. But when Billy Vail suggested this might mean their wanted chicken had flown the coop entire, Longarm was just as insistent that there were countless private carriage houses along the back alleys of the city, and that the mastermind behind all this infernal razzle-dazzle was as likely a city slicker as an old hermit dwelling in some cave in the Clearwater country.

When Vail suggested Longarm was just trying to get out of field work with the summer socials starting out at Cheeseman Park, his senior deputy managed, with some effort, not to blink. Though it was the simple truth that thanks to the sudden hunch about the job over Golden way Longarm had been paid, after all, and didn't really need the infernal travel allowance as much as he wanted some slap-and-tickle from that new gal at the Parthenon he'd been working on a good two weeks. But his conscience was clear as he paid attention to chores during the hours he was getting paid for and maybe a few hours a day extra, since that spunky little brunette at the Parthenon didn't get off before midnight, and only a damn fool waited for a gal that long with a beer schooner in his fist.

It made more sense, earlier in the evening, to check out Emma Gould, Ruth Jacobs and other notorious Denver madams, knowing they knew better than to fib to the law about big spenders with no visible means of support. But while that one still-unidentified gang member he'd first shot it out with had been packing way more money than any honest young gent had had the right to, the one still at large hadn't been spending free and easy in any local house of ill repute or, hell, the fancy men's shops along 16th Street.

Longarm was over closer to Cherry Creek, checking out a fancy saddler on Larimer near the just-about-sunset closing time, when he became aware he had a little shadow on his tail. She might not have been half as easy to spot in more prim and proper surroundings. But nice young ladies didn't stroll about on Larimer after dark any more than they might on Broadway in New York City. Denver's own Broadway was sort of dull and dark after business hours, but Larimer was where the visiting country boys looked for bright lights and flashier skirts than the one swishing after him now. He made certain he was still being followed by the reflection in a shut-down store before cutting abruptly east across the broad cobbled street, dodging a brewery dray coming one way and a coach and four the other. On the far side he consulted yet another plate-glass window, only to find that if anything the mysterious young gal had closed the gap between them a mite. She was wearing a dark straw boater with a veil, had on a dark dress a mite heavy for this time of the year, albeit Denver was almost always fairly cool after dark, summertime or not. So why in thunder was she carrying a *muff* as well? It never got *that* cool after dark in Denver between March and November.

He lit a cheroot to give himself time to study her reflection as he stood with his back to her. She stopped a few windows down to peer intently at the fertilizer sacks and farm tools of a closed hardware shop. She looked all wrong for a street walker and didn't make much more sense as a restless out-of-towner with a sense of adventure. He got his cheroot going good, gripped it in his teeth in unconscious imitation of a spooked pony, and whipped around the corner as if bolting somewhere important.

But then he flattened against the bricks on the darker side street, and when she sure enough came whipping around after him at almost a run, he just had to grab her, shove her face to the wall and relieve her of that mysterious muff before she knew what had happened.

Up close she was a downright pretty little thing with big brown eyes and light brown hair pinned up under her coffee-brown straw boater. She likely didn't usually stare quite so wide eyed at a man, and he felt sure she spoke more ladylike as a rule when she called him a murderous brute and dared him to kill her, too!

He told her to just hold her horses as he felt inside the oddly heavy muff to pull out a pearl-handled brass derringer, chambered to throw two rounds of .32 Short. He pocketed the nasty little weapon, handed back her muff, but said, "Now hold still with both your dainty fists against the bricks and your high-buttons spread just a mite wider, ma'am."

She protested she meant to do no such thing. So he told her, just as firmly albeit a heap softer, "We can have a police matron search you, stripped naked as a jay, if that's the way you want it, ma'am."

She placed both hands up against the bricks, one inside her muff, but her eyes were filled with tears as she begged him to inform her why he was arresting her so cruel.

He said, "I ain't sure I am yet. You can cease and desist them waterworks, you poor weeping little innocent. We both know who I am, at least, and it was your notion, not my own, to tail a peace officer with a concealed and lethal weapon."

As he began to put her down for more of the same she gasped and informed him, firmly, that he was insane as well as dirty if he expected to find another gun in or about her down *there*. But he just assured her, amiably, that women had been known to hide the damndest things in the damndest places. His now friendlier tone was occasioned by the fact that she had neither another weapon nor much else at all under her skirts. He enjoyed a more relaxed drag on his cheroot, glanced about to make sure they had that dark corner all to themselves, and said, "You can let go that brick wall, now. I might or might not give you your derringer back, empty. It all depends on the tale you have to tell me. So if I were you, I'd start at the beginning, Miss . . . ah?"

"Hayward, Kate Hayward," she replied. "I just this very afternoon identified my kid brother at the Denver Morgue. They told me a Deputy Custis Long was the one who back-shot him. Just now you were pointed out to me as one of the gents working out of the same office, and I've been trying to get up the nerve to approach you about the matter."

Longarm cocked an eyebrow and told her flatly, "Forget what I said about giving your gun back. Before I tell you just who I might be, in the unlikely event you might not know, which one of them at the morgue could you be related to, Miss Kate?"

She blinked her teary eyes and told him, "They had him toe-tagged as Jim Green, until I identified him for them this very sad day and, oh, what shall I ever tell our poor old parents?"

He repressed the impulse to whistle a few bars of the old ditty about being brung up by kind parents and told her instead, "It's just as well you didn't get to back-shoot me for back-shooting your kid brother, Miss Kate. For you'd have likely wound up really upsetting your parents, and I never done it. The one you may have noticed on the next

27

slab, a mite older with less left of his face right now, back-shot your brother when he, in turn, tried to give up sensible.''

He could see she didn't seem convinced. He told her, ''Whether you buy that or not, I'm taking down some facts and figures or I'm taking you in, Miss Kate. So we'd best find someplace with more light, where we can sit down comfortable for a considerable talk.''

She volunteered quickly, maybe a mite too quickly. ''We could go to my quarters. I live alone. So we won't be disturbed and it's only a short walk from here.''

Longarm didn't answer right off. There were times a man had to study on an answer to a lady's invite. His first thought was to ask her if she really thought he looked that stupid. For even if her tale of kid brothers and kind parents had a whiff of truth to it, old Samson had been mighty dumb to follow Delilah home, and old Delilah hadn't met up with Samson packing a concealed weapon.

On the other hand, he doubted he'd get much out of her acting like a sissy and he was packing three guns, counting her sneaky .32, himself. So to give himself more time to consider her offer he asked how far her place was and, when she said about a quarter mile, he figured he'd decide yes or no once they got there.

The quarters Kate Hayward said she'd rented above a carriage house off the alley running north and south between Curtis and Champa streets was really closer to half a mile than a quarter. So Longarm got the nuts and bolts of her sad story out of her along the way, making mental notes about loose screws here and there he meant to go over again with her, once he had his pencil and paper out.

The uncertainly lit neighborhood was almost if not quite as unfashionable as the one he could barely afford on the far side of Cherry Creek. It had recently been working-class residential. Then wholesale warehouses, lumberyards, brickyards and such had invaded to leave ragged clumps of frame housing along cinder-paved streets that got downright spooky after dark with most of the area deserted for the night. When they got to a dark alley entrance just east of Curtis and the gal seemed inclined to keep going, he took her gently but firmly by the elbow to say, "Hold on. Why circle around to the front if you say you hired yourself the top of an old carriage house? There has to be an alley entrance, right?"

She entered the alley with him. She had little choice in the matter, but repressed a shudder and complained, "It's so dark! I'm not sure I'll be able to find the place this way."

He soothed, "Just give me that number again. It's almost as dark out front and, well, to tell you the pure truth, I don't want your landlord or landlady peering through any side curtains at us as I carry you home."

She laughed uncertainly, and asked just what he feared anyone might suspect them of being up to. He told her, "I'm not worried about my own clear conscience, Miss Kate. I just hate to worry about what others might be planning to pull on me at times like this."

He steered her around some carelessly placed ashcans in the dark alley, adding, "If nobody knows I'm coming they can't be planning all that much. What was that number again and . . . Kee-rist! *Down!*"

She simply froze and would have gone on standing there if he hadn't swept her high-buttons out from under her with a sweep of his boot as he drew his .44-40 and fired.

His powerful six-gun's roar was drowned out by the double blast of a ten-gauge blasting number-nine buck through the space he and the girl would have been filling with their mortal clay if Longarm hadn't heard and identified the ominous snicks of two shotgun safeties, just in time.

Those same keen ears, honed by many a previous firefight

in the dark, told Longarm their assailant was making tracks to the south, alarmed if unharmed by Longarm firing even faster. The girl Longarm had rudely seated behind the ashcans seemed frozen by fear. He rolled back to his own feet, his double-action Colt still out, and hauled her up from the cinders with his free hand, muttering, "What's a nice gal like you doing in a shooting gallery like this?"

She didn't laugh. Her voice sounded like that of a little girl who'd been punished for something she'd never done as she informed him, "Someone just tried to hurt me!"

"I know. I was there. We can worry about who the intended target was later. First we have to make ourselves more scarce."

Suiting actions to words Longarm began by kicking a nearby fence of upright planks as hard as he could. He still had to kick it again before there was a slot wide enough to shove Kate through and then squeeze through after her. It was black as a bitch on the far side. When she asked where they were and why, he told her, "I hope we're in a lumberyard I recall as facing Curtis. Hold on, I want to reload and put my fool side arm away."

As he did so by feel in almost total darkness, they both heard a distant police whistle. She sounded as if that was a good thing to hear in this part of town, as she commented on it. He put his .44-40 away, took her by the arm again, and told her, "Right now I have enough on my plate. I was figuring on talking to you more private than I can generally manage in an infernal precinct house. So let's just eat this apple a bite at a time, starting with getting out of these parts, like I said."

Chapter 3

One of the more amusing things about Longarm's job, as a federal rather than local lawman, was that Uncle Sam left heaps of petty blue laws to the petty politicos who passed them. Hence Longarm felt free to herd the mysterious Miss Kate down yet two other dark alleyways and through the side door of an establishment his pals on the Denver P.D. were not supposed to even know about, it being their duty to shutdown such dens of vice and indecency.

As Longarm helped her up a dark and narrow flight of steps, she naturally asked where on earth they were and what that funny smell might be. He told her, "The place has no official name. It belongs to some Oriental folk I know. What you smell is opium. But don't you worry. Think of the place more like a vaudeville house than an opium den."

She murmured, "Oh, my Lord, I told Jimmy he was riding with a wild crowd, and now I'm in a durned old opium den with someone out to gun me, too!"

Longarm recalled that her dead kid brother over at the Denver Morgue had answered to James J. Hayward in life. So he didn't comment as he led her along a narrow corridor at the head of the stairs, found a door with a key in the lock, and opened it, murmuring, "This box is the one we want."

"We do? How come?" she asked dubiously as he led her into what seemed at first a tiny room furnished with an overstuffed sofa facing a far wall of velveteen drapes. He took off his Stetson, hung it on a handy brass hook, and pulled a cord to open the drapes halfway, just as she was asking where that music might be coming from. She gasped, ''Oh!'' and sat down, stunned, to take in the dimly lit show below, murmuring, ''I'd heard of places like this. I didn't know they really existed.''

Longarm gulped and confided, ''I wasn't expecting them to get so bawdy this early in the evening, ma'am. They usually just do sassy dances and such until midnight, with most of their duds on, I mean. I'd best shut these curtains so we won't be distracted while we talk.''

She was blushing rosy as she could get, but insisted, ''Not all the way. I confess I'm curious as to whether that couple down there on that bitty stage mean to go all the way and, well, it's not as if anyone can see *us* up here in this dark box, right?''

He smiled thinly and let the drawstring be as he sat down at her side, explaining, ''That's how come old Fong Kow *has* these sort of discreet boxes up here. The riffraff seated at the tables on the main floor don't care who sees 'em, doing what. But you could hardly expect fancy politicos and preachers to enjoy such goings on barefaced as cowhands and railroad men, if you follow my drift.''

She nodded and asked, ''How many other high-toned folk, like us, do you think there might be in the other private boxes up here, sir?''

He shrugged and said, ''I can't say for certain who else might or might not be up here with us, private and discreet. That's the way it's supposed to work. By the way, you can call me Custis if I get to call you Kate. Calling one another ma'am and sir seems a mite formal, considering.''

She giggled despite herself as she saw what the couple entertaining on the stage downstairs was up to at the moment. Then she covered her face with her hands, gasping, ''Oh, no! Have they no shame at all, and what am I *doing* in such a horrid place with a man I don't even know?''

He was saved from having to answer when the door behind them opened to admit a pretty little China doll bearing a tray. For as Longarm had known all along, one just couldn't get inside such an establishment without some member of the tong observing one's every move through all the infernal peepholes Orientals drilled through any wall less than two feet thick. He knew they knew that he knew he wouldn't be up here, with or without female companionship, if Fong Kow, or his tong at any rate, didn't approve of Longarm's sense of rough justice and the way he'd applied the same during the recent Chinese Riots stirred up by the loco labor leader, Dennis Kearney. So by tacit agreement Longarm would never be billed for this unofficial visit, and they'd naturally known he admired Maryland rye with his tea and fried noodles. But just in case he and the lady meant to stay a spell, someone downstairs had thought to include some meaty snacks with mustard and rye bread. Fong Kow was willing to meet the barbarians of the Golden Mountain halfway, as was evidenced by the couple rolling about onstage, downstairs, being white as the yahoos watching, and shouting rather ingenious suggestions for a proper grand finale to their sex act.

Some of their words were mighty rude. So Longarm poured spiked tea for both of them and placed the fried noodles handier to her than him as he said, "Well, so much for show business. Let's get back to how your kid brother was led astray."

He put the pot and his own cup to one side on the rosewood table between the sofa and the rail of their box. Then he shucked his frock coat while he was at it and hauled out his notebook and a stub pencil, adding, "I can remember most of what you've already told me. I just write down names and numbers. You say your kid brother left home a year or so ago and sent for you recent, saying he'd found a swell job here in Denver and . . . You got me sort of confused on that point, Kate. You said before

33

that the two of you were brung up by kind parents. Yet neither of you seemed anxious to dwell one moment longer than you had to under their swell roof in . . . Let's get that out of the way. Just where in what hometown might we be talking about?''

"Jimmy and me were born in Ogden," she said, "but then our folk moved up near Gooding, on the Snake River Plains.''

Longarm cocked an eyebrow, but it would have been dumb to ask if they were talking about Idaho Territory, albeit well south of the Clearwater country, so he just murmured, "I swear, you might have warned me you were a Mormon gal before I poured you forbidden tea and whiskey in one fool cup!''

She dimpled coyly at him and enjoyed a sip of what could have gotten her yelled at in Utah, explaining, "My parents were never observant Saints, even when they belonged to the Odgen Temple. But to tell the truth, our father could be mighty strict for a man who didn't think the rules applied to himself.''

She took another sip, glanced down at the stage to quickly look some other way when she saw who was down there now, and what they were up to. Then she said, "I didn't know my brother, Jimmy, was mixed up with any-thing *really* wicked, of course. He told me he was buying and selling stock down here, and when he sent me money to join him here in Denver—''

"I know about ambitious young gals with strict par-ents," he cut in. "Let's have the mailing address of your home spread.''

She sighed and said, "Just General Delivery, the Gooding post office, Custis. Dad gets in once or twice a month and . . . Oh, dear, we will have to tell them about what happened to Jimmy, won't we?''

He nodded soberly but said, "You could likely word things a heap more gentle, and it's not as if the boy is wanted by us now.''

He sipped some of his warm potent potion, put pencil back to paper, and said, "The boys he's been riding with still are. Unless that was just an escaped lunatic we met up with in the alley behind your quarters just now, someone's out to make a clean sweep of you Hayward kids. So I want you to study, tight, before you even consider covering up for anyone."

She stared saucer-eyed at him, demanding, "Why would anyone be after *me*? Wasn't it enough they got my poor kid brother killed?"

He shook his head and told her, "Nope. If the mastermind behind that last robbery attempt had been content to just let you mourn, he, she, or it wouldn't have sent someone to lay for you in that alley this evening."

She started to protest. He shushed her with a wave of his hand and insisted, "They weren't laying for *me* there. I'd have never been anywhere near that alley tonight if I hadn't been carrying you home."

She nodded, but said, "Wait, it couldn't have been me, either. I told you, before we ever entered that alley, that I meant to go in by way of the front of the lot, on Champa Street, remember?"

"Try her this way, then. Say your pal with a shotgun went to your hired carriage house, expecting to find you in at that hour. He or she would naturally use the back way."

She gasped, "Oh, Lord, that does work, if the killer was coming out just as we were coming in. But why, Custis? I swear I had no idea Jimmy was mixed up in anything crooked until I heard he'd been gunned the other day."

She was trembling, so it seemed only natural to put a comforting arm around her, and to hell with the notebook as he told her, "You never have told me how you knew your brother, or even anyone who could be related to you, might or might not be on view at the morgue this evening, Kate."

She nodded and said, "One of Jimmy's business partners told me, of course. He never said a word about Jimmy being shot by the law. He just told me something bad had happened and I found out the rest when I ran almost all the way and—''

''Back up,'' he cut in. ''The way we had it, your brother and his pals were boarding in another part of town entire, and they were keeping their matched buckskin ponies at a livery handy to the Golden Post Road. Your turn, Kate.''

She snuggled closer, as if for safety from a gathering storm, as she confided, ''Jimmy had rented the carriage house before he sent for me. He didn't stay there himself. It wouldn't have been decent, even if, or maybe because we were brother and sister. But naturally he came by for supper almost every night, and since you mention buckskin ponies, he and his friends did leave some down below me now and again.''

Longarm nodded thoughtfully and said, ''Now we're getting a heap warmer. Could you give me some names and describe the pals your kid brother brought home to supper, Kate?''

She shook her head and explained, ''They never joined us to break bread upstairs. Jimmy usually rode over alone, when he meant to set a spell. I only saw two of his business associates, as he liked to call them, when they all rode in together to put their ponies in the stalls down below and go somewhere else in the neighborhood afoot.''

He frowned so thoughtfully at that he failed to notice what the Mexican gent was doing to that gal on the stage below. But Kate had likely never seen such entertainment before, so she asked him, in a nervous whisper, ''Doesn't it hurt a girl when a man does that to her, Custis?''

He grimaced and replied, ''Speaking from more limited experience, I don't see how either of 'em could be getting much out of such an awkward position. They're just out to shock the rest of us, and I'd as soon talk about more serious sinning. You say these two nondescript owlhoots your brother rode buckskins with left 'em down below to sashay somewhere else in the neighborhood. There are all sorts of businesses and, dang it, other private homes someone could be using as a secret headquarters.''

Then he shot her a sharper look and added, "Hold on. You just told me one came by this afternoon to tell you personal that something had happened to your kid brother, Kate. Are you saying you never even looked his way?''

She almost snapped, "Of course I looked at him, you suspicious thing. I think his name was Walter something. He was a mite older than me, albeit a mite younger looking than you. He had dark blond hair and a sort of reddish mustache, not as bushy as your own.''

Longarm asked for more details and she continued, "He had on a blue denim jacket and jeans under a sort of mustard-tan hat, and his gun belt and center-fire saddle were silver mounted to match. I think he had the same sort of silver conchos on his hatband, now that I'm trying to picture him harder. When he told me they had a dead boy at the morgue that could well be my poor Jimmy, I confess I didn't stop to admire his infernal looks!''

Longarm patted her shoulder soothingly and asked about any mount said saddle might have been aboard. She shrugged and answered, "Just a buckskin cow pony, the same as Jimmy rode. I remember asking him one time how come he and his pals all seemed to have bought ponies from the same litter. He said they'd gotten a good price off some breeder who went in for buckskins.''

Longarm nodded soberly and decided, "He may have been telling you the truth. Then again, that center-fire saddle the one cuss favored reads more Arizona or West Coast than Idaho, to me.''

She brightened and said, "Oh, the one called Walter did say he hailed from Idaho Territory, like Jimmy and me, now that I think back to a less exciting few words we exchanged when he first came by with my brother and their other pal. I never spoke to that one at all. He was dark featured and sort of sulky shy, the way some breeds act. I think they called him Gus.''

Longarm almost let that go by him. Then he blinked and asked her, ''Does the name Gus Arquette ring any bells in your pretty little head?''

She shook the head in question to ask him who they might be talking about. He told her, ''A longer romp around Robin Hood's barn than I was planning on, cuss my luck. If you and your brother hailed from Idaho Territory, and the one called Walter said he was from up yonder, then tossing in a breed who could be Gus Junior to a gent who breeds buckskin cayuses up Idaho way does add up to some serious snooping. Only, damn it, at least one would-be robber we didn't get has to be somewhere down *here*. The one who just tried to shut you up forever with that shotgun adds up to at least *two* gang members in or about the fair city of Denver!''

''Couldn't Walter have laid for me all that time, after telling me about Jimmy being in the morgue?'' she asked.

He shook his head firmly and explained, ''Not if old Walter has brain-one. Had he never pestered you at all it might have taken us all a heap longer to figure out who we had over at the morgue and, meanwhile, old Walter could have been long gone.''

She stared past him at the stage below to murmur sort of wistfully, ''He might have changed his mind after telling me. He might have tore over to my quarters without taking time to consider. Then it might have struck him harder, as you just allowed, he had lots of time to run off to other parts if only I wasn't around to point him out as a gent my brother had ridden with.''

Longarm insisted, ''It works better as orders from some smarter albeit meaner mastermind. You said before that the boys left their mounts with your brother's and visited someone in the neighborhood.''

She nodded, but went on staring over the rail in fascination as, down below, the heroic-breasted redhead now onstage played a game of rapid-fire stoop-tag atop a muscular gent chosen more for size than any indication of intellect. Kate asked Longarm sort of husky toned, "How do you suppose he's able to control his passion like that? Look at him! He's not even breathing hard!"

Longarm shrugged and assured her, "The redhead's breathing hard enough for the both of them. That old boy likely has to get good and drunk before he can act so silly in front of so many folk. I know I would."

"He can't be too drunk," she insisted. "He's hung like a stud horse and showing every inch of it stiff as a poker!"

Longarm gulped and replied, "I can't see every inch of anything, thanks to the way his more activated pard seems content to take it. Do we have to talk dirty about them lowlifes, Kate? I only brung you here because it was the nearest safe cover. It's not as if we have you out of the woods entirely yet. There's at least one cuss with a weapon more serious than that old boy's out to do you a heap dirtier with it and, damn it, we don't even know *why*, let alone *who*! Did you get a good look at the other one they had over at the morgue with your brother, the one identified as a Mr. Black?"

She nodded and said, "He wasn't the one called Gus or Walter, of course. I'd never seen him before. Oh, good heavens! Look what that shameless redhead is doing to him now!"

He did. It was sort of frustrating to watch such an undeserving cuss study French. He grimaced and insisted, "Pay attention, Kate. If you're sure the one I nailed just after he back-shot your kid brother was neither the blond kid called Walter nor the breed they called Gus, Walter and Gus are still with us. Do you have anything of real value in your quarters above that carriage house, honey?"

She shrugged and told him, "I arrived in Denver with

little more than the clothes on my back and the money Jimmy had sent me. I fear the money's about spent and—Oh, look! He's finally gotten on top of her and, my heavens, he does seem to be making up for lost time!''

Longarm got wearily to his feet, stepped over to the door, and turned the key in the lock. As he rejoined her on the sofa, Kate asked why. He told her, ''If the help here feels the door's been locked on the inside, they don't come in to empty the ashtrays and such.'' Then he reeled her in for a good firm kiss.

She kissed back as firmly, but as he ran his free hand up under her skirts she tried to cross her silk-sheathed legs, protesting, ''Whatever are you searching me for now, sir?''

He chuckled fondly but saw no need to insult a lady by informing her he suspected he knew why she'd run off from strict parents with a wayward kid brother. He assured himself, as his questing fingers got to smooth naked flesh above her frilly garters and kept roaming, that he owed it to them both to get it over with and clear their fool heads for more important studies. So the next thing she knew—for he'd known right off what he was doing—Kate had the insteps of her wide-spread high-buttons hooked on the rail of their private box and he was kneeling between her open thighs with his pants and gun rig down in order to get up her private parts with his own old organ grinder. Kate gasped as she felt him enter her and then, as she clung to his shirt-clad torso, staring over his shoulder at the naked couple down below, she moaned, ''Oh, Jesus! Do you think anyone in the boxes across the way can see what we're doing, darling?''

He asked her if she could see what anyone might be doing across the way. She sounded almost disappointed as she moaned, ''No. They could be behaving as badly as we are, even with those curtains wide open, and you couldn't tell from here.''

''There you go. Do you want me to draw our curtains so we can get even badder?''

To which she replied with a hiss of pure lust, "Don't you dare! I've never done anything as wicked as this before and I love it! Let me slide these stuffy clothes off over my head, but for God's sake don't stop!"

He didn't. It would have hurt like fire to try, and as she got out of everything but her high-buttons and black silk stockings without making him miss a stroke he was glad the curtains were wide open, too. He couldn't see the show going on behind his back in this position, but the soft warm lamplight from the ceiling fixtures of the theater showed him just what he was getting into himself, and unlike some gals with pretty faces and not much else to offer, Kate Hayward was pretty all over, even posed in such a way, with her eyes clamped shut and her bare breasts flushed and glowing with raw passion.

She climaxed ahead of him. He wasn't far behind. As she felt him ejaculating in her still-pulsating love pit she sighed and murmured, "Oh, that was lovely, darling. If only life's fleeting pleasures didn't have to end so soon!"

He thrust teasingly, assuring her, "Speak for yourself, you sweet little thing. I dasn't take you back to your place, now that some rascal's gunning for you there. But I do know a swell little hotel just about a block and a half from here and I, for one, would like to get my own duds off entire."

She began to move her hips on the edge of the sofa again, as she murmured, "Go ahead and strip, then. You surely can't expect me to check into a hotel with a man I'm not engaged to!"

He moved his own hips in time with her teasing gyrations, as any man would have had to by then, but insisted, "Let's not talk dumb, doll. Someone's out to shut you up for good and, well, seeing we've opened you up so fine, it makes more sense for us to sort of, well, hang out together."

She hugged him closer and nibbled one of his earlobes as she assured him in a husky whisper, "You just go

41

ahead and let it all hang out in me, darling. Just don't ask me to shack up with you in any infernal house of assignation, as if I was a bad girl!''

He started to ask her what she thought they were up to at the moment, but then it was all the way up and it didn't feel bad at all. By the time they'd stripped him down to just his own socks and he was shoving it to her dog-style as she gripped the rail and stared down at the fat lady treating her Irish wolfhound in the same friendly fashion, Longarm had grown weary of debating morals with anyone as contrary on the subject as this wild little gal. Kate was one of those unfortunate, or maybe fortunate, sex maniacs who seemed to feel sensible slap-and-tickle in total privacy had to be sneaky and dirty. Yet during a tobacco break on the sofa between their almost public displays, hidden only by the shadows high above the leering lowlifes down below, Kate confided coyly that she'd lost her virtue in church, with a choirboy in the organ loft, with the organ playing ''Rock of Ages'' all around them in the dimly lit heights above the congregation.

He assured her it sounded like fun. But in truth his heart just wasn't in it. As a lawman he'd dealt too often with the grim aftereffects of indiscreet and doubtless less than comfortable ruttings.

He told her, ''Fun is fun, and being only human I've been known to take dumb chances in pursuit of the same, Kate. But we're not talking about shocking more prudish folk right now. There's at least one son of a bitch out to catch us in the act or any damned way he or she can! Can't you see that?''

She dropped to her knees on the rug in front of him, replying, ''That door is locked and your six-gun's handy, honey-bunch. What I can't see is all of this sweet stuff hard as I like it, or why you keep saying another *lady* could be after me. Jimmy never once mentioned any women associated with his business here in town.''

He shrugged his bare shoulders and replied, "He didn't mention pulling robberies on sudden ponies, either. My point is that we don't know beans about what we're up against and— Jesus, watch those damned *teeth*!"

She said she would, on condition he put it up her some more, and while that was not an unpleasant chore so far, it wasn't getting one lick earlier, and as he brought her to climax again he said so, adding, "This infernal sofa just ain't big enough for both of us, if we mean to catch a wink of sleep tonight, Kate. So about that hotel just down the way . . ."

But she insisted, "No, no, a thousand times no! Only bad girls go to hotels with men." And when he pointed out how naughty some might say they'd just been she just laughed, sort of naughty, and assured him it was all right to go to a theater with a man and not the fault of any lady if her escort got a mite forward during the show.

He sighed and said, "All right, you win, I'll just carry you to that safe hotel and check you in as a single. I want to sneak back to scout your carriage house, once I fort you safe, in any case."

It sounded reasonable enough to him. But she objected, even as she rubbed against him like a naked kitten, "You're just trying to get me up in that wicked hotel room with you, you big sneak. I know how men fib to girls just to have their own way with 'em."

He laughed incredulously and said, "Suffering snakes, I've just *had* my wicked way with you, unless it was vice versa. Be sensible, Kate. We can't spend the night here on this one skinny sofa with all that rough laughter and such going on 'til dawn or later."

She asked why not. He groped for his discarded vest, fumbled out a cheroot, and told her, "Because it's just plain dumb and downright uncomfortable." He lit his smoke. She didn't notice what else he was up to, at first. But when she did she asked him in a little-girl voice how come he seemed to be getting dressed.

43

He growled, "When I can't get a mule or a woman to move it makes as much sense to just dismount and move my own fool ass where I got to get it. You ought to be safe enough here if you lock the door after me. Don't open it to anyone else. I ought to be back this side of midnight, and we can argue some more about the best way two grown adults can best sleep aboard a bitty sofa only meant for casual loving."

She almost wailed, "But where will you be while I'm stuck here all alone, on or off this damned sofa, you brute?"

"I told you. I want to scout your quarters. I'd rather use a key than pick your lock. So seeing we've learned to treat one another so true, I'll trust you with your derringer if you'll trust me with the key to your quarters."

She agreed but wanted to tag along. He told her she couldn't, and they were still arguing when he ducked out in the corridor, waited 'til he'd heard her reluctantly lock up after him, and eased down and out of the nameless establishment, shaking his head in wonder at the contrary notions of womankind.

For he knew that should he live to be a hundred he'd never savvy the way the gears meshed in their pretty little heads. Old Kate was willing to screw him silly in the shadows of a theater box, likely just as willing to follow him down a dark alley into yet another ambush, but she flat-out refused to let him bed her comfortable in a safe and secure hotel room.

He didn't know whether to be glad or sad that he just couldn't think about slap-and-tickle like a female. For it seemed mighty obvious he and most other men were missing something.

Chapter 4

It seemed unlikely anyone could have been crouched out
back in the alley with that shotgun all this time. Nonethe-
less, Longarm chose a more prudent approach via Champa
Street. As he strode up from the corner, squinting for
house numbers in the tricky light, he considered how Kate
had intended to take this very route home before he'd
persuaded her the alley offered them a shortcut.

So how come they'd almost wound up with their faces
full of number-nine buck? The would-be killer should have
known Kate usually came in by the front way, assuming
she'd been the intended target.

Picking himself as the intended target didn't work a lick
better. Nobody had had any reason to expect him to show
up, either way. But who else was left, once you eliminated
both intended victims?

He found the modest frame dwelling the carriage house
had been built out back for. Kate had told him her brother
had hired the quarters out back total, free to come and go
as they pleased. If the old-timers who owned the property
owned a carriage, or had any other use for a carriage
house, it seemed dubious they'd have ever rented it to
strangers to begin with.

The backyard was even darker. Although Longarm's
eyes were now about as adjusted to the night as they could
get, he still had a time finding his way in. He was helped a
heap by simply knowing the way most carriage houses
were laid out in these parts.

Folk who still kept their own horses and carriages in this no-longer-fashionable part of town could drive in from the front, to let others out near the house, or out via the back alley if that should be their fancy. Thus most carriage houses, including this one, had big sliding doors, front and back, with servants' quarters, or rooms to let, on the second floor. Some such structures had a small side door with a separate stairwell leading topside. But in other cases, such as this particular one, you got upstairs from the no-nonsense bottom, likely by way of a cross between a flight of stairs and a ladder.

The big sliding door facing the back of the house wasn't locked. Longarm took a deep breath, slid it open just wide enough, and eased through the narrow slit with his gun out, then slid his back along the pitch-black inner surface of the door before he slid it shut with a thud, the odds as even as he could manage.

He almost fired blind at a faint creak of leather just off to his left. He was glad he'd dropped to one knee, instead, when he heard the sleepy horse over that way shift its weight again and give a soft curious snort. He was tempted to snort back. But while most ponies were prone to snort in the dark at strangers, he knew they might not have as much to say about their own riders, should any still be around. So the question before the house now was just how many players there might be in this particular game of blindman's buff. Asking out loud for someone to explain the rules could add up to suicide. On the other hand, he knew he was going to feel mighty dumb if he crouched here like a nervous nelly until the cold gray dawn explained he was all alone in here with no more than a nervous pony.

It was the pony that had him so proddy. Kate hadn't mentioned keeping a mount of her own below her quarters. The mounts her kid brother and that other young owlhoot had been riding had been rounded up. At least one gang member, more likely two, still had to be accounted for. But, suffering snakes, what sort of mounted moron would still be lurking about the quarters of a known sidekick's sister at this late date?

Sweeping the brick-paved floor with his free fingers as he knelt there in the darkness, Longarm encountered lots of straw stems and a rusty horseshoe nail. He pegged it into a far corner. The pony tethered off to his left, stomped a hoof and asked why, in horse lingo. But no human beings on or about the premises seemed to fall for the old night-fighting ruse. Another standard ruse was to just lie doggo until the other cuss ran out of notions and decided to chance you not being there. Longarm had come close to making that fatal move once, during the war. The other raw recruit had broken cover first. It was the sort of experience that stayed with a man.

Longarm pegged a dry horse apple into another corner of the dark cavernous carriage house. It sounded like a fairly convincing boot-heel clunk to him. But not even the mysterious pony seemed to buy it. The critter seemed to be getting used to Longarm's company, as well as any other still lurking about.

There was always another way to skin a cat. Longarm fumbled out his notebook and a waterproof match, left-handed, but not without some modest skill. He gingerly and silently formed a paper ball around the match stem. Then he silently rose to full height and braced himself to crab either way before he simply thumbnailed the match head aflame and tossed his improvised fireball the hell away from him, firing his six-gun, thrice, at his first glimpse of the other man hunkered in a far corner, clad all in blue denim and holding a shotgun across his infernal knees!

The impact of Longarm's well-aimed rounds jarred the mysterious figure visibly but failed to spill him from his corner. So Longarm shot him again as the feeble flame flickered out. The paper had burned long enough to let

Longarm get his bearings in the unfamiliar surroundings, though. So he had a lantern going and was reloading his .44-40 by the time the first police whistles tweeted in the distance. They'd had a city ordinance about gunfire in downtown Denver for some time now. He didn't care. As a lawman he was allowed to gun owlhoots anywhere he found 'em, and on rare occasions the local P.D. could be sort of helpful.

This evening turned out to be one such occasion. For although Longarm had had plenty of time to get a handle on the now illuminated scene, he was even more puzzled by the time a brace of copper badges he knew of old came rapping on the lit-up alley-side window with their night sticks. Longarm slid the alley door open to let them both in, saying, "Evening, Kevin. Howdy, Pat. You boys came to the right place. That was me you just heard shooting so late at night."

As the two Irish beat pounders stepped inside, the one called Kevin spotted the body propped up in that one corner. So he gave a soft whistle and said, "We figured someone had to be dead as soon as we saw it was you through that darling little window."

His partner strode over to the one stall with a horse's rump sticking out of it, observing, "A buckskin cow pony this would be, just like Sergeant Nolan told us to be keeping an eye peeled to be sighting!"

Longarm nodded and said, "Still saddled and bridled, as well as branded Double Tipi. I'd say the gent in yonder corner had some unfinished business here."

He brought them both up to date on his reasons for shooting up total strangers in carriage houses, leaving out the dirty parts about old Kate, but allowing she was a material witness the gang was likely out to silence for keeps. They didn't argue. So he left them in charge of the live cayuse and dead rider as he went up the narrow stairway to the still-dark second floor.

There wasn't anything half as interesting up there, even after he'd lit the lamp next to Kate's bed. He found nothing in the way of travel baggage. Some obviously new as well as inexpensive toilet articles lay atop a mirrored washstand. He slipped them in the side pockets of his frock coat. Kate had said she'd just shown up and there seemed no reason for her to ever come back here, now. He meant to send her on home to her kinfolk, if possible, or failing that, at least somewhere her late brother's fellow crooks couldn't find her. Their motive was commencing to make more sense now. The one down below was neither a breed nor possessed of a red or any other sort of mustache. They'd sent someone Kate likely couldn't identify to make certain she never identified the gang members she *had* seen in her brother's company.

He went back down, feeling maybe a mite satisfied now that things were starting to make more sense. But then the patrolman called Pat spoiled it all by saying, "There's something we're not clear about here, Longarm. Sure, we just heard you firing your grand .44-40 and you just told us you were shooting it at this very villain, but, to put it delicate as we can, we don't see how things could have happened as you say."

Longarm shrugged and answered, "I usually call things the way I see 'em, boys. How do you say you see things here?"

The one called Kevin pointed with his billy at the oddly positioned corpse in the corner, saying, "It's stiff as a plank he'd be, and in God's truth I've never seen rigor mortis set in so suddenly."

Pat said, in a more certain tone, "Neither have I, and I fought at Shiloh, where many a boy wound up stiff before it was over and all."

Longarm muttered, "I noticed," as he stepped between them with a puzzled frown. He hunkered down for a closer look. He could see where his four rounds of .44-40 had punched neat bloodless holes in the dead man's light-blue shirt. When Longarm tried to take the ten-gauge shotgun from the lifeless hands they refused to let go. He rocked the cadaver back and forth, using the shotgun as his lever, before he nodded soberly and announced, "You boys are right. It seems I just shot me a dead man, the more fool me."

He thought back to the early exchange of fire out in the alley as he took his watch out of a vest pocket to check the exact time. He'd met up with Kate Hayward just after sundown. It had felt a heap longer but it didn't seem to be midnight, yet. He mused aloud, half to himself, "Say an ambusher in an alley got hit in the back as he turned away. Say he ran for his pony, felt too poorly to mount up and ride out, and just hunkered in a corner a spell, hoping he'd feel better in the sweet by and by."

The copper badge called Kevin shrugged and said, "Heart attack victims do that all the time. If they ain't smart enough to call the doctor, someone's sure to call us, later. But this old boy's been dead a spell and then *moved*, Longarm."

Longarm started to ask a dumb question. Then he got back to his feet and stepped back to regard the oddly posed cadaver in an overall general way before he nodded and said, "You're sure to make the detective squad at the rate you're going, old son. For until you pointed it out I hadn't noticed how flat he seemed to one side."

Kevin smiled smugly and observed, "Cats do that when they lie dead a time before someone's after kicking them against a fence with the flat side up. I'd say this gentleman lay curled on one side a good while, don't ask me where, and then someone sat him up in that corner, wedged firm enough to sit tight through a fusillade, and then—"

"And then we'd best see what the coroner's forensic crew has to tell us about him," Longarm cut in firmly, his mind grasshoppering to cover more than one bet. "You boys know the routine, here. I have to go fetch another witness. What say we all meet at the morgue by one A.M.?''

They neither agreed nor disagreed, for Longarm was already going out the back door, his mind in a whirl as he stomped off down the alley, cussing himself. For even if Billy Vail hadn't told him, more than once, he'd told his fool self as often not to screw any women he might have to appear in court against.

He didn't see how good old Kate could have gunned a sidekick of her brother and then gone scouting for a law-man to bring home with her to view the remains. Nobody already dead could have fired that ten-gauge at either of them in any case. But on the other hand there had to be more than one ten-gauge in this wicked world and the whole damned gang seemed to wear the same outfits and ride the same cayuse buckskins off the same spread.

Worse yet, Kate had sort of established herself as a wild young gal who didn't think along exactly logical lines. He decided it made as much sense to just question her as it might to just guess at what she might or might not have been up to all the time her kid brother was off getting his own wild self killed.

But when he got back to Fong Kow's he found the key in the lock *outside* the door he'd left old Kate behind. He popped it open anyway, hoping against hope, but of course she wasn't there, and when he finally caught up with old Fong Kow, smoking plain old tobacco in the cellar by his safe, the skinny old cuss couldn't even make an edu-cated guess as to when Kate might have left, on her own or maybe against her will.

Longarm had it figured long before he got to the office the next morning, but Billy Vail still felt honor-bound to inform him the trail had grown colder than a banker's heart, and old Billy didn't know the half of it, since Longarm wasn't inclined to kiss and tell.

51

In bringing his boss up to date on the misadventures of the evening past, Longarm had only said a kinswoman of at least one dead outlaw had come forward, but that her story had just a few holes in it and he just couldn't say where she might or might not be at the moment. He didn't see how it mattered, one way or the other, what a great as well as easy lay old Kate was. She'd told him the truth or she'd fed him a bushel of lies and, either way, there seemed no way to verify or trip her up unless and until he had some notion where in thunder she'd run off to.

Billy Vail agreed it seemed a mite shitty to put out a federal want on a young lady who'd been good enough to come forward and was likely only running scared, now that associates of her dead brother had treated her so surly. Vail said, ''If she just lit out for parts unknown, neither them nor us is likely to bother her no more. On the other hand, if she's run for home, them outlaws might have her late brother's mailing address. So you'd best give it to me and I'll wire the sheriff up yonder to keep an eye on, or at least out for, the poor little gal and her more decent kinfolk.''

Longarm nodded and got out his notebook. Then he blinked down at it in dismay and muttered, ''Shit! I must have torn that leaf out last night, to light that paper flare I told you about!''

Before Vail could call him a total asshole he quickly added, ''She said they hailed from Gooding County, Idaho Territory, and . . . right, they had a spread outside the county seat and came in now and again to pick up their mail in care of General Delivery.''

Vail looked slightly mollified as he growled, ''Good. Hayward is a less usual name than Smith or Jones, and someone up yonder ought to recall a Mama Hayward, a Papa Hayward, and their two damned kids, even if neither has ever been reported as a runaway to the local law.''

He wrote himself a memo and leaned back to relight his

morning cigar, squinting at the mental map in his canny old head a spell before he told Longarm, "I know where Gooding is. It's just down the Snake from Twin Falls. You can get to Twin Falls via the north division of the Union Pacific, changing at Granger. Lord only knows how you'll ever get a direct connection up to Orofino in the Clearwater country, so you may as well commence your mission down around Gooding on the Snake and, even if you don't find that lady witness at home, some of the neighbors might be able to put you on her outlaw brother's back trail."

Longarm reached for a cheroot as he protested, "Billy, Jimmy Hayward's over in the Denver Morgue with a couple of his business associates, even as we speak, and the Snake River Plains are at least a week's ride south of that half-Cayuse horse breeder up around Orofino."

Vail blew an octopus cloud of pungent blue smoke at Longarm as he replied, "I wish you'd pay attention to your elders. I know full well that at least four desperados who got this far aboard buckskins bred by old Gus Arquette in the Clearwater country are no longer with us. As far as we know, however, that infernal old breed is still breeding sawed-off but sudden race horses up near Orofino."

"You told me not to arrest Arquette!" Longarm cut in, blowing smoke right back at Vail.

"I just now told you to pay attention, my child. I know we dasn't arrest Arquette as things now stand. Without proof he's been knowingly behaving as a remount service to half the young owlhoots west of the Big Muddy, he'd beat us in court for sure and likely alert all the others to how smart we are. All they'd have to do, even if they didn't want to shut the old breed breeder up, would be to just change the way they've been operating a mite. You know how sneaky some crooks are. Do I have to draw you a damned picture?"

Longarm grimaced and said, "No, and I wish you'd

blow that smoke some other direction, Billy. What are you smoking these days, an old feather mattress spoiled by pissing in bed?''

He blew some of his less reeky as well as less expensive smoke out his nostrils and added, "I've been wondering why a gang that size has stuck to the same methods half this long. I mean, sure, it might make it tougher to I.D. a particular gang member, later, with all the victims describing everyone the same, from feed-sack mask to identical mount. But after that things commence to work in favor of the law, Billy. We'd have never figured out we were dealing with widely scattered three-man details from the same sort of private cavalry, had their leader or leaders failed to outfit them all so uniform.''

Vail nodded soberly and observed, "Their quartermaster crook must like to buy in bulk. My point is that once they take to riding horses of another color—''

"I follow your drift," Longarm cut in with a weary sigh. "In sum, you want me to pussyfoot discreet until I can get a line on just who might have picked up a considerable remuda of nearly identical ponies from the Clearwater country. Do I have to wear this sissy tweed suit? Up yonder in such rugged country it's sure to stand out about as barefaced as a bigger badge than I like to show off.''

Vail started to object. Department regulations were department regulations, and President Hayes even frowned on federal employees *drinking* on their own damned time. But old Billy Vail had started out in the pre-war West, where a gent who got a shave and a haircut once a year had been considered a hell of an improvement over many a good old boy. So he said, indulgently, "I reckon you'd fade in better, dressed more cow than courthouse. Now about the nearest government remount station, up on the Snake River Plains—''

"That'd be Fort Hall," Longarm cut in. "It's a mite out of the way to begin with, and you know how neither Army nor Indian agents part with good ponies, save at gunpoint. I figured on selecting the best of those cayuse buckskins we've recovered from the gang. Running a pony all that way by rail may slow me a mite. I know I won't meet as many pretty ladies riding on a freight train, but . . .''

"You've been mixing loco weed with your tobacco!" Vail snorted in disgust, waving his own stinky smoke like a baton. "No matter which pony off the Double Tipi spread you might choose, the son of a bitching cayuse will be branded local as well as prominent! What in thunder are you going to say when, not if, some nosy rider up to the Clearwater country asks you just how you came by such a distinguished mount?''

Longarm smiled thinly and replied, with a sort of wolfish gleam in his gun-muzzle-gray eyes, "Ain't sure, yet. I reckon it'll sort of depend on who asks, as well as how polite.''

Vail protested, "Damn it, old son, riding a dead man's pony into his own damned stomping grounds could be just begging for trouble.''

"I just said that, boss. If you don't want me tangling with crooks, don't send me after none.''

Chapter 5

Getting to Gooding from Denver was a complicated pain in the ass and, once Longarm got there with his chosen cayuse and more personal possibles, he wasn't too sure he'd gotten anywhere.

Idaho Territory was one of those afterthoughts laid out on a mostly blank survey map by politicians who'd never been there. In this particular case the Congress back East had decided Oregon, Montana, or maybe both looked a mite big for their britches on the map. So they'd drawn some fresh lines resulting in the fresh territories of Washington and Idaho. Save for using the Continental Divide for some, not all, of Idaho's eastern border, they hadn't paid attention to the geographic features of the real northwest in slicing it up with a straight edge at long range. So the political divisions had little to do with the way things were, unless one wanted to count the political confusion occasioned by sticking a mess of folk with nothing else in common under a single territorial government.

The recently incorporated county and county seat of Gooding lay spread out fairly flat on the Snake River Plain of southern Idaho, which should have been included with Utah, according to most of the mostly Mormon settlers living there, or considered part of the eastern Oregon desert, if one asked the Indian minority left. For in their shining times the Bannock, Shoshone and such hadn't noticed any lines drawn with straight edges across the sage flats they roamed with the pronghorn and jackass rabbit.

The Indians everywhere else in Idaho were as different as the flora, fauna, and more alpine scenery. But Longarm knew he had to deal with this unusually flat part of Idaho first and allowed himself to be more amused than worried about the way his own kind had named the whole territory, dumb, after a Shoshone clan the early mountain men had sort of insulted by translating their totem as ''snake'' when the Indians had meant ''salmon.''

Longarm was only reminded of the above when he detrained at Gooding, left the pony he'd left in the town livery, along with his possibles, for now, and ambled on over to the small frame public library near the schoolhouse. He was supposed to pay a courtesy call on the local law before he pestered any local folk, he knew. But he also knew a lawman in strange surroundings could sometimes save himself a heap of legwork if he boned up on the community he was visiting, and that small-town libraries were just busting with local history, ofttimes printed at private expense by ''early settlers,'' meaning anyone who'd been in town long enough to vote, this far west. For most Americans tended to be as awestruck by a hundred years as Europeans might be by a thousand and, to the amusement of European travelers, seemed anxious to record the events of ten years past lest they be lost to history forever.

Knowing all this, Longarm strode into the bitty library to ask the bitty brunette librarian if they had any tomes on local geneology. She regarded him dubiously through her wire-framed specs. For they were all alone in the place, here in the middle of the afternoon with school out for summer and all the kids old enough to read working at their chores if they knew what was good for them. Worse yet, he could tell just by looking at her starched midi blouse and prim pink lips, they could both see he was dressed sort of casual for a student of even local history.

He hadn't gotten around to shaving yet, after sharing a boxcar with his cayuse and some other livestock in his faded blue denims and gray hickory shirt.

But she was sport enough to ask him just which local family he meant to read up on. So he told her, "I'd best deal all my cards straight up, ma'am. I answer to Custis Long and I ride for Uncle Sam as a U.S. deputy marshal. I'm here in Gooding to enlighten as well as question some of your local citizenry. I doubt I'll get to arrest anyone you might know. I seldom get that lucky. How do you like it so far?"

She must have liked it enough to let her tight lips relax a tad softer. It was one hell of an improvement, even if she didn't outright smile at him when she said this was just about the most exciting event she'd ever had any part in since she'd come to Gooding almost two whole years ago. She said, "I fear we don't have any published histories of local families here, although the Mormons go in for that a lot. You might be able to get them to cooperate with the federal government at their temple near the depot."

He made a mental note that the Latter-day Saints, as they preferred to be called, couldn't be running Gooding entire, if this gentile gal got to run the town library. Knowing he was on safe ground, some Mormons still being sensitive as memories of the Mormon Wars slowly faded, he told her, "I'm interested in one family that sort of started out as Saints, but dropped out. Their name would be Hayward. I doubt the temple library would have them on any honor roll, but they do seem to have been early settlers in these parts. So might you have a modest tome on just how and when Gooding township got started, ma'am?"

She said, "My friends call me Trisha and I know what you mean. I believe someone told me the town was named after some army captain, unless he was a beaver trapper. The territory itself, as they now teach in the school across

59

the way, was named for Indian words meaning something like, 'Behold, the sun is coming down the mountain,' unless it means something like there being light upon the mountain. There seems to be some argument. But at any rate, don't you think it sounds just grand?''

He smiled thinly and replied, ''Downright poetical, had any real Indian ever said it. I happen to know a few words of Ho, as the Bannock, Shoshone, Paiute and such refer to themselves. It was our notion, not their own, to divide Indians of the same nation into so-called tribes. Ida means salmon, and Ho, like I just said, means people.''

She looked mighty unconvinced as she demanded, ''Are you trying to tell me Idaho simply means Salmon People?''

To which he felt obliged to reply, ''I ain't trying. I'm telling. It gets even dumber when you consider the so-called Snake River to our south. It was named after the same Salmon People clan of the Shoshone Nation by the same so-called translator for the old Lewis and Clark expedition. I know all this for the simple reason I had to scout for the army during that Shoshone uprising a few years back and we sure had a heap of dumb remarks about Snake Indians in our army manuals.''

She shook her head as if to clear it, saying, ''Excuse me, sir, but I seem to be missing something. What on earth could the Snake Indians along the Snake River have to do with sunlight coming down the mountain?''

He sighed and said, ''You're right. You weren't paying attention. Lewis and Clark hired themselves some French Canadian trappers from way east of the Shining Mountains, or Rockies, to guide them over the same. They had a Shoshone gal along who naturally spoke her own Ho lingo. Her name was Bird Woman and they spelled it wrong as Sacagawea, later on, after it was all over and they'd figured out they should have listened to her.''

Trisha brightened and said, ''Oh, I read about Sacagawea

and how she guided the Lewis and Clark expedition when I was in school.''

He grimaced and said, ''The Indians tell it different. Like I said, it was later on that they figured their camp drudge and pass-about play-pretty knew more than the rest of 'em put together about the country she'd been kidnapped from as a girl-child. As they kept trending west, the country getting ever more familiar to her, Bird Woman started searching for her kin, the Salmon People of the Shoshone. The whites noticed she always made the same hand sign for her clan, a wig-wag motion meant to imitate a swimming salmon. Only it worked as well, to their eyes, as a snake wriggling through the grass. So when they *did* encounter Bird Woman's Ida Ho, among the headwaters of a mighty westbound river, they put them down as Snake Indians. That worked fine until later mountain men who paid more attention described the very same folk as Shoshone, and nobody could figure out what had ever happened to the Snakes, see?''

She said, ''Not really. It so happens there *is* a Salmon River just to the north. How come nobody named that the Snake River if you're so smart?''

He smiled sheepishly and replied, ''I never said I was smart. I only said some early explorers were dumb. By the time anyone found the Salmon River they already had a Snake River on the map. So this time they paid more attention to the local Indians, and it ain't as if *any* river draining west to the Pacific has a monopoly on salmon, by the way. The Indians along the Salmon were Ida Ho as well.''

He suddenly caught himself getting set to drone on about Indians when Billy Vail had sent him after a breed at best, and raised both hands in a mock gesture of surrender, saying, ''Hold your fire, Miss Trisha. The question before the house is how many white folk named Hayward might be left in these parts, and where I'm supposed to look for them. Might you at least have a township directory on hand?''

She did, and watched with interest as he cracked it open in vain for even an odd spelling of the name Kate Hayward had given him as that of her strict and likely more truthful parents.

The petite brunette who'd never claimed to know anyone by that name suggested, ''We can't have nearly all the names of all the new settlers who've moved in since the coming of the railroad.''

But he shook his head and explained, ''I was told they came up here from Ogden, likely by wagon, after giving Utah Territory a whirl and deciding they liked coffee with their breakfasts after all.''

She dimpled and said, ''They may have found the Mormon church tithes more bothersome. Most of the lapsed Mormons I know dropped out to avoid temple tithes. Imagine anyone having to surrender ten percent of all they earn! It's un-American!''

He had to reply, ''It does sound steep. We American folk had to fire that King George when he demanded that two-and-a-half percent tax that time. But to tell the truth I ain't up here collecting taxes. Unless they tell me different over at your post office, I'm going to have to call yet another pretty lady a big fibber. For she distinctly told me her name was Kate Hayward and that both she and her brother, Jimmy, were off a family spread up here in Gooding County. Why do you suppose an otherwise sweet enough little thing would want to lie so barefaced to a friendly cuss like me?''

The librarian shrugged and answered, ''Maybe she just never wanted you to come calling. I know it sounds mean, but I've been known to play that trick at a grange dance in my time.''

He chuckled, allowed he saw no reason to doubt that, and made as if to leave. But then, in a more hopeful tone,

Trisha suggested, "You might want to come back around closing time, say six. For I'd be proud to mention that name, Kate Hayward, to one and all who might stop by this afternoon. You say she's pretty, and sort of wild?"

He answered firmly, "I never say how wild or not wild a lady may be, Miss Trisha. I can't even say for sure she was lying when she told me she hailed from these parts. If my job was that easy I'd never get to ride or even walk in so many circles. But I thank you for your helpful suggestion and I'll be back this evening, Lord willing and the creeks don't rise."

She dimpled at him to demand, "What if you find the information you seek somewhere else, in the meantime?"

"I'll still be back. I ain't half as dumb as I may look."

Being the county seat, the town rated a post office as well as a railroad depot, but neither amounted to anything much larger than a chicken coop. The postmaster was an old-timer who opened up between trains and kept the place padlocked whenever he had to help an engine crew jerk boiler water. Neither job paid all that much, but together they added up to a decent living, the old man said.

Longarm said he knew how a man had to keep his wits about him to get by in such a cruel uncaring world, and after they'd jawed about other such important matters a spell Longarm brought up the matter of the Hayward family, and whether they might or might not pick up any mail, General Delivery or otherwise.

The old-timer started to shake his head. Then he brightened and said, "Hold on, I suspect I got a letter addressed to some cuss by that name, if only I could recall where I put it."

He turned his back to Longarm, rummaged through his pigeonholes longer than Longarm felt like waiting, only to turn around and say, "Someone must have picked it up. I only recalled it because it came in an envelope with an

63

impressive return address. Some government office sent them Haywards a fat old letter calling for three cents instead of two.''

Longarm tried, ''Might that letter have been from Marshal William Vail of the Denver District Court, sir?''

The old-timer answered, ''That sounds about right and, hell, you don't have to call me sir. Everyone in these parts calls me Casper. The only thing I can't abide is Pop. That other name, Vail, sounds about right for that officious letter. I've no idea what it could have been about, of course.''

Longarm said, ''That's all right. I've a pretty good notion, and I wasn't looking forward to breaking the news to them, myself.''

He reached under his denim jacket for two cheroots as he asked, ''I don't suppose you might remember just when some member of the Hayward clan came by for their mail, or what he or she might have looked like, Casper?''

The old man shook his head, saying, ''It ain't slow, like this, all the time. Folk come at me in bunches when I first open up in the morning or after a train comes through. It's the trains as drop off the mail sacks, you see.''

Longarm handed him a smoke, anyway, saying, ''Well, at least we know some damned body claimed the letter my office sent addressed to James Hayward, General Delivery.''

He might have said more. But just as he was striking a light for the two of them the door behind him opened and a voice said, flatly but not unkindly, ''Go ahead and light that cheroot before you burn yourself. But get both hands up as you turn about slow and respectable, stranger!''

Longarm did as he was told. It seemed the sensible response, even if that was only a broom handle someone had shoved against his left kidney. As he slowly turned, lit cheroot gripped in a friendly smile and both hands cupped at shoulder level, he noticed it had been a twelve-gauge prodding at his back, and that the gent still covering his balls with it, point blank, was sporting a mail-order badge of nickel-plate brass on the checked shirt he was trying to burst open with an overly ample gut. Longarm nodded at the badge and said, "Howdy, Marshal. Before you blow my balls off, I'd best inform you we're on the same side. Would you be willing to hold your fire if I was to reach inside this jacket for my own badge and billfold?"

The Gooding law stared dubiously at the stubble on Longarm's chin as he replied, "Let's study on it a mite. That cross-draw double-action on your hip hangs sort of gunslick, no offense, and it just so happens you answer to an all-points night letter we just got from the Justice Department. They tell me, over to the livery, you was the one as stabled that buckskin cayuse, branded sort of sinister, and there was mention of an all denim summer outfit as well."

Longarm nodded and tried, "You likely got that night letter from my very own boss, U.S. Marshal Billy Vail. The reason I chose me such a frisky mount is that I'm trying to cut the trail of a whole heap of owlhoots mounted the same sudden way. Mine's branded Double Tipi because we shot one of the gang off it, down by Denver."

The town law still seemed to have some reservations as he softly asked, "Would you say it sounded smart for a lawman to dress the same way as them mysterious cayuse-riding blue boys?"

To which Longarm replied, more certainly, "I wasn't expecting another lawman to get the drop on me this far from where I'm really bound. My boss suspects and I tend to agree the outfit we're after originated up in the Clearwater country. We know their remuda was bred on one stud spread up near Orofino. I was hoping someone less law-abiding might comment on my mount and denim jacket somewhere along the way. You know how tough it can be to start a conversation with strangers, even when they don't know anything."

The strange lawman pointing a shotgun at his crotch pursed his lips thoughtfully and decided, "You're either the brass-balled liar of the west or commencing to make just a mite of sense. Have you been paying attention back there, Casper?"

The old-timer on the far side of the counter allowed he'd found the whole conversation mighty interesting, as a matter of fact, and added, "I don't reckon he's a bandit, Chuck. He was talking decent enough to me when you come in with that fool scattergun."

But Chuck, if that was what he liked to be called, just told the older man to reach over and around to see what their mysterious visitor might or might not have in the way of I.D.

Things got a heap friendlier once Chuck had taken a good gander at Longarm's more impressive badge and personal identification. Chuck lowered the muzzle of his twelve-gauge, handed the billfold back to its owner, and allowed, with a curt nod, "I've heard of a deputy marshal named Long as specializes in far-flung cases a mite tougher than most. If you'd be Longarm, I'm glad to know you and anxious to help in any way I can. But didn't you just say you hope to cut the trail of them stickup artists well to the north, in the Clearwaters?"

Longarm said it was more complicated than that, as he put away his billfold and dropped his arms. So Chuck suggested they go jaw about it over some suds at the Sage Grouse Saloon, just up the way. Longarm agreed that was the nicest thing anyone had said to him since he and his pony had gotten off at Gooding. It was nobody else's business whether that librarian was just flirting for the practice or not.

It still being business hours on a weekday, the saloon was almost empty as well as pleasantly cool and gloomy at this hour. Thanks to the altitude and resultant thin air, the Snake River Plains were only heat-stroke-hot where the dry sunlight could get right at you, even in high summer. The two lawmen took a pitcher of draft and a couple of clay mugs to a deserted corner table and got down to getting to know one another better.

The town law confided how unwise it was for parents named Wagner to sprinkle a son Charles if they didn't want him to be called Chuck Wagner for the rest of his fool life. Longarm said he'd call his new pal Charley and assured him Custis was a mighty dumb thing to dub a kid. When asked where in thunder they'd come up with a name like Custis, Longarm was forced to confide, "Martha Washington's first husband. Being called Custis must have drove him to an early grave. I suspect someone way back on our family tree might have been related. Custis was the handle of a fine old Virginia family and we wound up in West-by-God Virginia, some fool way."

He sipped some beer, found it a mite flat but refreshingly cool, and added, "It could have been worse. Some of them First Families of Virginia had mighty odd handles. I'm glad nobody named me Peabody Long. Cowhand humor can get sort of earthy."

Wagner chuckled at the thought of a poor soul saddled with a name like Piss Potty and so, seeing he had the local law in a better mood, Longarm tried, "Hayward is the unsual name I'm trying to scout up here in your neck of the woods, Charley. I don't suppose you've ever come across it?"

Chuck Wagner didn't look friendly at all as he replied, in a growl, "The hell you say. The old lady was decent enough, I reckon, before she died the winter before last. Old Jim Hayward's a shiftless trash-white with a drinking problem and his kids were worse, before we run 'em out of the county."

Longarm frowned thoughtfully down into his suds, murmuring, "That ain't exactly the tale at least one of the

Hayward kids told me just a few nights back. Let's hear your version, Charley.''

The pudgy local lawman shrugged and replied, ''Hell, there's not all that much to tell. Once you dub hardscrabble homesteaders as trash-whites you've about said it all. I can't say it's true they got drummed out of the Mormon temple, down Utah way, for forgetting what the Prophet Joseph had to say about sipping anything sinful as tea. I do know the old rummy made up for any previous deprivation by arriving in Idaho Territory drunk, and staying that way to the best of his ability ever since.''

Longarm nodded grimly and said, ''I get the picture. What can you tell me about the two kids, Kate and Jimmy junior?''

Wagner swallowed some beer, lowered his mug, and smiled sort of wistfully as he said, ''The gal was a looker and, some say, no better than she should have been, albeit I can't say I ever got any, my ownself. Her kid brother was a rat-faced sneak thief. They'd both earned a reputation here in town for thievery, only she stole bolder and lied her way out of it pretty good whenever she got caught. She didn't get caught as often as Jimmy. He was a hopeless case. Like I tell my own kids, a kid has to grow up slick or honest. There's just no way for a dumb thief to get by in this world.''

Longarm didn't really need more stale lager. So he leaned back to light another smoke before he said, ''You're right. Young Jimmy Hayward was gunned by one of his own when he tried to surrender the first time he was under serious fire. I met his sister later. Just before someone tried to blow her away in the wake of her dead brother.''

Chuck Wagner seemed mighty interested, so Longarm brought him up to date, leaving out the part about old Kate treating him so friendly just before she ran out on him without a word of explanation. He did tell the other lawman she'd done that, however, so Wagner nodded and said, "They say she ran off easy. More than once when she was a schoolgirl and her mother was still alive. She never got far, bitty white gals being sort of rare out on the sage flats, no matter what their story, so her mother could keep her out of real trouble, while the poor woman was still alive."

The pudgy lawman stared off into space with a dreamy little smile to add, "Lord have mercy, there was just no holding her the last couple of years, after her mother went under and her daddy was too drunk to notice. They caught her doing it in church, with a poor old gray-haired preacher man! And leave us not forget the time she offered to screw the judge, in his chambers, if he'd just forget those shop-lifting charges against her."

Longarm grimaced, sincerely ashamed of his own weak nature, as Wagner went on to relate how a stronger willed or maybe not as virile circuit judge had decided it made more sense, all in all, to just run both the damned Hayward kids out of town.

Longarm blinked and said, "Hold on. You say Kate and her kid brother rode out of Gooding on the same rail, Charley?"

Wagner shook his head and explained, "That wouldn't have been constitutional. You can't just out and out order an undesirable to leave town. You got to be delicate if you don't want some pesky lawyer swearing out fool writs at you."

Longarm nodded impatiently, and said, "I know how it's done. I ran Soapy Smith out of Denver a spell back for the good of all concerned. Spare me the details and let me have some dates I can tally up."

Wagner tried. He thought hard and decided, "I never saw hide nor hair of either, after I sent word out to their spread. I had a line rider I sometimes deputize for posse riding drop by with an informal message to the effect I meant to arrest either Kate or Jimmy, the next time I seen either in town, with or without anyone else's property in their infernal sticky fingers. I didn't see either leave. I doubt they wanted me to. But it's my understanding Jimmy lit out right after I sent word. The gal, Kate, moped about the spread through last winter, according to some kiss-and-tell cowhands. I saw no reason to go after her as long as she stayed the hell out on the range. I can't say for sure when she finally caught a train to Denver. But we know she did because she borrowed the money for her ticket, promising to send it back as soon as she got some dinero from her prosperous brother in the big city. I told the sweet old schoolmarm she swindled that I doubted Colorado would send her back to us on such a dubious charge. Anyone dumb enough to loan money to a Hayward deserves to lose it, but like I said, she was a sweet old gal, along with being downright stupid.''

Longarm got out his notebook, asking for the victim's name and address. Chuck Wagner scowled and growled, ''Forget it! I don't want you putting more tears in a dear old lady's eyes, Longarm. There's nothing she can tell you that I can't. Kate Hayward studied with the poor old spinster gal, when she wasn't playing skirts-up hooky in the sagebrush, weather permitting and anyone in pants being willing.''

''She was wild as that?'' sighed Longarm, resisting an urge to haul out his old ring-dang-do for a short-arm inspection.

The local who seemed to have known Kate longer, if not as well in the biblical sense, decided, ''Well, she might not have really sucked off that cowhand through a bob-wire fence. It sounds suspiciously like that trail herding song and you know how folk talk about a gal, once they get to talking at all. But she did get that preacher man defrocked and she lied so much that, like the little boy as cried wolf, there was just no telling what she might or might not have been up to in her short but all-too-long stay with us.''

Longarm didn't feel any less ashamed of himself as he took down directions to the wanton young gal's home spread. It was getting a mite late to ride out there now. He had time to study on whether he really wanted to do so at all. If Billy Vail had already informed the poor old cuss his only son was dead and that the Denver Morgue was waiting on funeral instructions there was little anyone could add, save the fact his only daughter gave swell blow jobs. But Longarm recorded the way out to the Hayward home spread anyway. He still didn't know enough for sure to take anything for granted and, while Chuck Wagner's words made old Kate out as a compulsive fibber who couldn't even level with folk out to help her, it was still the word of one stranger he didn't really know against that of a sweet little thing whose only fault was a sort of impulsive nature.

If only he could figure out how come she'd cut out on him like that, if she had cut out and hadn't been kidnapped or worse by the gang her kid brother had gone wrong with or . . . hell, someone else entire!

Chapter 6

As Longarm had hoped and as cow-town custom almost required by statute law, the barber down the block from the Sage Grouse Saloon had bathtubs for hire in the back. So Longarm got a fresh shirt and underdrawers from his possibles roll in the livery tack room and paid the damned barber the damned two-bits for running a tub full of what looked and felt like tepid tea.

But at least rusty water didn't leave a man reeking of musty hay, railroad smoke or horseshit and, once he'd bathed, bought a shave, and told the barber to trim his mustache less ferocious, he even allowed himself to be splashed with sissy-smelling toilet water.

He knew a certain amount of boxcar riding still had to be stuck to his duds. But more important, he'd seldom met a small-time barber who didn't gossip like an old biddy, albeit more accurate, as a rule, since half the menfolk in town passed through at least every other month, and men in general gossiped more accurate, if just as spiteful, as the unfair sex.

But if Chuck Wagner had a local rep for bullshitting, neither the long-winded barber nor the half dozen other customers Longarm met going in or coming out were sore enough at him to say so in front of strangers in town. It being an election year, Longarm found it easy enough to bring the subject of local officials up. But the boys in and about Gooding seemed about to reelect the same court-

73

house gang and didn't seem to shoot nervous glances over their shoulders as they said so, calm and sort of small-town smug. It hardly seemed likely the gang young Jimmy Hayward had ridden with could have originated in these parts in any case. But lest Billy Vail ever chide him about leaving any such stone unturned, Longarm brought the subject of banditry aboard cayuse ponies to their attention as he bought some after-shave cheroots from the barber with his change and lit one up.

He saw he'd wasted money, the greedy barber selling the same brand two for a nickel where most tobacco shops offered you three. For his question was replied to with sincerely curious stares. One old geezer with a drinker's nose allowed he'd heard some talk about a big gang dressed and mounted all the same, operating in other parts, praise Jesus. When Longarm mentioned buckskin cayuse ponies branded Double Tipi they all seemed to agree there was no such brand registered with Gooding County or likely any-where else on the Snake River Plains. The name of Gaston, or Gus, Arquette evoked not a flicker of interest. To make sure they weren't just dullards, Longarm tossed the handle of Jimmy Hayward Junior into the ring.

That woke 'em up. All but one stockman who allowed he was a Saint who didn't get into town all that much had tales to tell of Jimmy junior and his wayward habits. They made him sound like one of those natural cutups, craving admiration or at least attention until their hell-raising got them put away for good in prison or a potter's field. When Longarm told them the kid had been killed down Denver way, the kindest comment anyone there had to say was, "I hope the little shit died gut-shot."

Yet looking back on his barbershop conversation as he signed himself into the one hotel near the depot, Longarm couldn't recall anyone but Chuck Wagner having a bad word to say about the bad boy's sister, Kate. Yet Chuck had admitted he'd mostly gone by local gossip instead of personal knowledge.

The skinny bald room clerk asked if he'd like to go on up to his hired room right off. Longarm shook his head and replied, "I'll take your word there's six bits' worth of room upstairs and that it'll still be there when and if I get back. Aside from it not being suppertime yet, I might get lucky. But you'd best hand me the key, now, in case I don't."

The clerk didn't argue that point. Some greenhorned traveling men didn't know it, and room clerks seldom admitted it, but once they knew you were good for the money it saved time and trouble for all concerned if a hotel guest simply packed his own damned key instead of pausing at the desk every time he went in or out. But as Longarm pocketed the key to the room he'd hired sight unseen, the clerk felt obliged to ask how come he'd hired the room at all if he'd meant that last casual remark the way it had sounded to yet another man of the world.

Longarm saw he still had plenty of time to kill. So he confided, "Far be it from me to gossip about the ladies of your fair city, pard. But since you say you've been to the fair and back, have you ever noticed how good they are at reading our simple minds, and how contrary they can act when they know, and they always seem to, that you've burned even one bridge behind you?"

The older man of the world sighed and said, "Lord love 'em, don't I ever! I mind this time down in Salt Lake City when I was sure as hell tonight was the night and told my roommate him and his gal could have the full private use of the place and— Well, I reckon you know who got to spend the wee small hours setting on a park bench across from the Mormon Temple."

Then he brightened and added, "I follow your drift. You figure as long as you have a soft bed and snug room of your own to come home to, she won't want to turn you into a pumpkin at midnight, right?"

Longarm smiled sheepishly and replied, "I ain't quite

that superstitious. None of us would ever have to sleep alone if things were half that certain. But I've found it's better to be safe than sorry, and I've been stuck after midnight with no place to go, just like every other man who wasn't born an unromantic priss.''

They shook on it and Longarm went to scout up an early supper. He ate light at the chili parlor he wound up in, knowing he might get fed as well as fondled if he'd read the smoke signals in that librarian's big blue eyes half right. On the other hand, he knew he could be wrong, so he topped his one bowl of chili con carne with just one serving of mince pie and a couple of mugs of black coffee. He knew he'd want to stay awake a spell no matter how things turned out at the library.

As he ambled on over to it, he kept warning himself not to get his hopes up enough to cause real pain if little Trisha had only been flirting or, hell, gone home early. Then he laughed at himself as he saw he *was* being superstitious. He'd read in some book that primitives like himself and some Indians believed in something the professors called Negative Magic. They tried to make things come out the way they wanted by the casting of reverse spells, such as muttering, ''I bet I miss,'' after betting their last penny on not missing. Longarm had done that, just like everyone else, but he liked to think of himself as logical, and it was simply a fact that librarians, schoolmarms and farmers' daughters got more hard up than barmaids or waitress gals, who got more offers in a day than some gals could hope for in a year.

He naturally behaved himself at the Denver Library whenever he indulged his secret vice of curiosity by reading up on clock repair or seamanship. But he'd often found in his tumbleweed travels that library gals came in two distinct varieties, not counting what they looked like, and Trisha hadn't struck him as the kind who hissed at folk to hush and sent back any books with kissing in 'em as just too dirty to abide. So she was likely the other kind, who read a lot and likely didn't get too many chances to satisfy her curiosity. He made up his mind to see if they had any books by Virginia Woodhull or Oscar Wilde in stock, before he walked her home, if he got to walk her home.

"Calm down, you damn fool!" he muttered to himself, adding in a barely audible growl, "it won't be the end of the world, either way, and we got to ride on in the cold gray dawn in any case."

But when he got there, to find her alone, with her reading specs put away and her big blue eyes staring sweet and myopic, he knew he'd just never forgive himself if he never even got to kiss anything that swell.

She looked as if she was glad to see him, too. She said, "You'll never guess who I got to gossip with about that horrid Kate Hayward this afternoon, Custis!"

He said that was for certain, unless she wanted to tell him. So she said, "Miss Maxine Pratt, from the schoolhouse across the way. School just let out for the summer so she's been catching up on her reading and, well, in sum, she told me Kate Hayward had been one of her students and that one night she'd come by, all teary eyed, and the next thing Miss Maxine knew she'd loaned the wicked thing a month's salary, on her promise to pay it back, that is."

Longarm nodded soberly and said, "That bears out what your town law told me this very afternoon. I noticed the time I met up with Kate Hayward in Denver that she spoke mighty convincing, even when she wasn't making too much sense."

The hopefully more truthful librarian said, "That's what poor Miss Maxine said. She said that even though the girl had been a holy terror as a student she managed to convince her old teacher that she'd turned out ladylike after all. But why don't we let Miss Maxine tell you all about it herself? She lives right next door to the schoolhouse and it's only a hop, skip and jump away."

Longarm wanted to meet up with an old spinster
schoolmarm about as much as he wanted to dig postholes,
and the one who'd first said three could be a crowd hadn't
even seen this particular blue-eyed brunette by the soft
light of gloaming. But he knew, that as in the case of a
gent showing up with no place else to go, later, gals took
refusal to meet one of their pals as a premature attack on
their fair white flesh. So he said he'd be proud to carry her
over to the infernal pain-in-the-ass schoolmarm's.

As she pinned a perky straw boater atop her swept-up
wavy black hair, she didn't need any further formal
preparations to step out of doors, it being summer on the
Snake River Plains. He waited while she locked up, then
offered her his elbow but let her do the steering as she led
him the way he didn't really want to go. He figured her
true intentions involved presenting him for inspection and
perhaps the approval of an older chum. He knew no older
gal with one lick of envy or, hell, common sense, was
about to advise this one to indulge any man born of mortal
woman in one sweet night of no-strings amour.

But Longarm liked to consider himself a good sport and
so, as he studied on it, he had to wonder if it might not be
best for all concerned to toss this one back in the creek of
carnal desire. For small-town gals who took a passing-
through lover serious enough to introduce him around
town could wind up feeling used and abused in the cold
gray dawn that just couldn't be avoided unless he meant to
quit his job.

So when they got to the cottonwood-shaded cottage in
the tricky evening light, Longarm wasn't paying all that
much attention to even Trisha's perfume when the schoolmarm Kate Hayward had swindled opened up as if she'd
been expecting company and bade them come right in. It
was only after she'd seated them on a big leather davenport in her front parlor and told them the coffee was almost
ready that he noticed, by the orange and purple light

coming in through her lace curtains, how dumb she'd been described to him.

For, sure, she had to be older than him, or at least prematured a mite. But it hardly seemed fair to call anyone an old lady when there was only a white streak in her otherwise raven hair and she was hourglassing so inspiring inside her blouse and skirt. If she had any more wrinkles than he had they didn't show in such soft light. Her eyes, unlike those of the younger and skinnier brunette, were dark as an Apache's, albeit a lot friendlier. The high cheekbones of her heart-shaped face made him wonder if she could have some Indian blood, way back. Her ivory complexion told him it would have to be way back indeed. It wouldn't have been polite to ask her if she was white entire, so he never.

The effect was marred just a mite when their gracious hostess asked Longarm if he'd be kind enough to light the lamps while she fetched the coffee and cake. He lit two, one at either end of the long chesterfield. She didn't seem to mind when she came back to set her big tray down on the bitty tea table in front of them, and then set herself down between Longarm and Trisha to pour, or keep them the hell apart. She had a way of looking right at a man, as if she could read his mind, and that he'd best just keep his fool thoughts proper if he knew what was good for him. He knew she'd likely learned that trick from teaching the kids of rustic settler folk. It hardly seemed possible she'd been Kate Hayward's schoolmarm, as mature as Kate seemed to be acting of late. But when he studied her over the rim of his cup in the crueler light of coal oil, he could see her fine-boned face had been etched a mite by time and a climate that just didn't care how anything animal, vege-table or even mineral stood up to 'em. He decided he liked her better for being so brave about the way things just had to be. He knew even older looking gals who tried to fool everyone with low-trimmed lamps, rice powder and hair dye. He almost blurted out how downright tempting she still looked, no matter how damned old she'd gotten. But on reflection he doubted she'd want to hear how others had described her as a poor old thing. They'd no doubt simply known her a spell in country where things kept changing so sudden that events of five or ten years past seemed ancient history. So he asked her, instead, to tell him how that sassy Kate Hayward they both knew had swindled her.

Old Maxine heaved a sad little chuckle and replied, "It was as much my own fault as that poor troubled child's, looking back on it after managing to pay my own bills after all. I hadn't seen her for a time. She'd simply stopped coming to school after I'd been forced to flunk her in the seventh grade. So when she showed up, about this time of an evening, more mature in every way—"

"Hold on, Miss Maxine," Longarm cut in with a puzzled frown, "how old a young lady could we be talking about? Don't most kids make it to the seventh grade at around the age of twelve?"

The wayward Kate Hayward's former teacher nodded but explained, "She flunked more than once. Partly but not solely through no fault of her own. She and her younger brother had a good ride into town, and once their mother came down with consumption, long before she found her way on to the promised land, there was simply no one out there firm enough, or tough enough, to get such willful students off to school, even in clement weather."

She sliced and served a rich chocolate cake to go with the fine Arbuckle coffee she'd made, adding, "I suppose our willful Kate dropped out of school at about sixteen or seventeen. It must have felt awkward to her, trying to compete with twelve-year-olds, and losing. It wasn't as if she didn't have any brains. She and that terrible little brother, Jimmy, simply refused to apply them to anything that looked at all like work."

He said he'd had to arrest a heap of folk with that

attitude in his time, and when she added Kate Hayward
had come to her for that train fare a good three or four
years after quitting school, he felt a lot better, knowing he
wouldn't have to arrest himself for messing with too young
a gal. As he let her pour him more washdown, it was that
sort of cake, he was content to just listen without cross-
examination, for in sum her tale of woe was simple enough
to him. He'd had Kate tell him things sincere. Maxine
Pratt told him, "I think what helped her pull the wool over
my eyes was the way she mixed fibs I had no way of
tripping her up on with things I knew to be true. I had
heard her younger brother had run off under a cloud and I
suppose it made me feel good to hear he'd made something of himself down Denver way. I knew Kate had made
a lot of enemies here in town and I felt that whether she
deserved her bad name or not it couldn't be much fun, or
even safe, for a young girl to be living alone out there with
such a dirty old man. You see, James Hayward Senior had
as bad a reputation as both his offspring put together."

On the far side of her, the younger Trisha gasped, "Oh,
Maxine, what a horrid thing to say! The old man is the
girl's own father!"

Maxine shrugged and answered simply, "It happens.
Neither father nor daughter have ever been nominated for
canonization, and where does one expect a drunken cattle
thief to draw the line? The old man's not that old and the
girl was amoral as well as very pretty."

"Don't talk so dirty in mixed company!" the young
librarian insisted. "I can't abide dirty talk, even when
there's a chance it could be true, and I know for a fact that
Mr. Hayward is over forty years old, so how could he,
even if he was half that wicked?"

The schoolmarm tried not to smile as she calmly met
Longarm's eye. The effect was sort of Mona Lisa. It was
all he could do not to bust out laughing. He said, "Let's
just agree you didn't feel the young lady was exposed to

81

wholesome influences. Chuck Wagner told me she'd been told she'd best leave town. There's no argument that she did. For I just met her down in Denver. Only she told me her kid brother had sent her the money to get there.''

The swindled schoolmarm shrugged and replied, ''Maybe he did. She was wearing a store-bought dress that looked brand new when she showed up weeping on my doorstep. I just admitted she played me for a fool. They say she took that preacher for a pretty penny, not to press charges, years ago, when he deflowered her in the choir loft, or so she said. I swear I don't know how I could have lost track of what a wild and wicked teenager she'd been, but we live and learn.''

Before Longarm could ask his next question the furiously flushed librarian on old Maxine's far side sprang to her feet to fluster down at them both, ''If I hear one more word half so sinful I swear I'll just go home, so there!''

Maxine smiled up at Trisha, sort of motherly, to tell her, ''Oh, for heaven's sake calm down, child. We're talking to a lawman about a whole clan of no-good trash. If any of them had the morals of a Digger Indian we might not be talking about them at all.'' Then, as if to make sure he wound up red-faced, too, she turned to Longarm to ask him if that wasn't the simple truth.

He nodded soberly, and replied for both of them to hear, ''Folk prone to abide by the Ten Commandments seldom wind up in jail, let alone the Denver Morgue, like young Jimmy Hayward. But Miss Trisha has a good point. I'm not out to arrest Kate Hayward, as far as I know. So her morals or lack of the same don't matter to me all that much.''

Trisha began to sit back down as Longarm continued, ''It's the wild ways of her kid brother I'm really back-tracking. We know he went badder than his older sister, whether she knew all he was up to or not. So, seeing as you used to teach him, or try to, what can you tell me about any other young rascals he might have run a mite wild with, before Chuck Wagner ran him out of town, Miss Maxine?''

She wrinkled her nose and explained, ''It wouldn't be fair to say any of the other boys Jimmy Hayward led into temptation now and again were half as wicked as he or even his sister was. He never ran or rode with what you might call a tough local gang, if that's what you mean.''

Longarm said it was and added, ''He must have taken up with that bunch of buckskin pony riders later, then. The way they say bitty Billy the Kid joined up with other young toughs after getting run out of Silver City, solo.''

Trisha chimed in brightly, ''Oh, do you think Jimmy Hayward could be mixed up with the notorious Billy the Kid, Custis? I've been reading a lot about that bunch of late!''

Longarm grimaced and replied, ''Small wonder, the way the newspapers tell tall tales about The Kid, Frank and Jesse, and other shiftless rascals we ain't caught up with yet. I doubt the gang I'm after could be tied in with the James boys or that poor half-wit known as Henry McCarthy, Kid Antrim, William Bonney or Billy the Whatever. For one thing, the mastermind Jimmy Hayward was riding for seems sort of smart.''

Trisha tried, ''Well, Billy the Kid must be pretty slick if he's still at large this evening, right?''

To which Longarm had to reply with a laugh, ''Suffering snakes, not hardly. The Kid had a pardon offered to him for the taking, after anyone could see the side he was riding for had lost. Even as we speak he could light out for anywhere but New Mexico Territory and likely never get caught. The one official photograph they have of him ain't him, if I'm half right about the one time I suspected we may have met up, friendly.''

He sipped more coffee, aware that chocolate cake made a man's mouth mighty dry in such thin Idaho air, and added,

"The fool kid they call Billy won't even leave the Valley of the Pecos and, big as it may be, they're sure to nail him if he don't. I suspect he can't abide going somewhere he's not well known, and sort of feared. He's a sort of harmless looking little squirt. Way smaller than Jimmy Hayward or, come to study on it, his older sister, Kate. But let's stick to Jimmy and his confederates still at large. You say he led some other local boys into temptation, Miss Maxine?"

She nodded but said, "Nothing to indicate any of them are sticking people up these days. Both the Hayward kids as well as their father were accused, often enough, of stealing anything from a lace kerchief to unbranded livestock. But as a schoolboy Jimmy never got anyone to steal anything important. You know how boys are at that silly age between a little fuzz on the lip and real hair where it counts."

He did. So he didn't answer. But Trisha gasped, "Maxine! For heaven's sake!"

Her somewhat older and certainly more worldly chum shrugged and said, "Oh, grow up, dear. We both know boys that age write words like f.u.c.k. on outhouse walls whether they know what they mean or not. Isn't that true, Custis?"

Longarm didn't answer. He didn't know what he was supposed to say. Trisha did. She sprang back up, wailing like a banshee, to dash out of the parlor and hit the front door running. By the time Longarm could get to his feet, grab his hat, and follow, she was long gone. He stood there in the doorway, staring out at the darkness for an awkward spell. Then he shrugged and went back in to where Maxine was calmly pouring from a bottle instead of a coffeepot. As he rejoined her on the chesterfield she told him, "I thought we'd have a little brandy in our coffee, now that we seem to have separated the adults from the children."

He put his hat aside again, cocking one eyebrow as he

84

asked her soberly, "Were you really trying to get rid of her, you sly little thing?"

She just smiled like Mona Lisa some more and started to pour brandy in his cup. He told her, "No thanks, ma'am. There are times to imbibe strong drink and there are times a man needs his wits about him. I ain't sure this would be a good time to get me drunk."

To which she replied demurely, "Speak for yourself, then. It's been a while for me, and I fear I'm going to have to get pretty blotto to get us from here to, ah, wherever you want to go with me."

But when Longarm pivoted to trim the lamp at his end of her davenport she still felt obliged to fluster, "Not so fast, sir! Didn't you hear what I just said?"

To which he replied by taking her in his arms to tell her, "Getting drunk to make love makes no more sense than puffing on an unlit pipe to save on one's tobacco bill. Anything worth doing deserves to be done clear headed, honey."

But when he kissed her she struggled in his arms, protesting it was damn it way too early and that all sorts of townsfolk might still be on the street outside right now, with no more than a lace curtain across that front window to guard her good name from pure scandal.

So he reached across her, lowering her junoesque torso to the leather cushions as he had to, to get at the other lamp, and once the room was dark, save for soft moonbeams through those same lace curtains, she kissed back with more enthusiasm, until she felt him hauling up her skirts and protested, "Stop that, you fresh thing. I'm not wearing anything under that summer-weight calico!"

He'd already noticed this much. She had a heap of nice soft skin above her knee socks, and there was a lot to be said for a lady letting herself go to full figure, as long as she didn't overdo it, and old Maxine hadn't. For had all of her ample thighs been solid muscle he'd have had a hell of

85

a time wedging them apart as he rolled atop her, and then where would they have been?

As it was, she moaned and begged for him to stop, even as he got his gun rig off and his soft denim duds out of the way, albeit barely. As he moved up a mite to improve his aim, Maxine laughed lewdly despite herself and insisted, "Damn it, Custis, we're both too old for this teenager groping about on a damned sofa!"

Then he felt himself entering her and, as he entered her yet more she sobbed, "Oh, yesss! There's a lot to be said for puppy love after all, as long as it's with a sly old dog with a full-grown petter!"

He petted her, inside and out, as best he knew how while she rolled her head back and forth, letting her hair come unpinned and making scandalous suggestions as he pounded her to glory. He knew she was going to beat him over the moon, and he knew how some gals who got carried away with wild words and wriggles tended to feel as soon as they'd had their wicked way with a poor innocent youth. So he was braced for it, and kept going, almost there himself, when she all of a sudden went limp under him, started to cry, and pleaded with him to stop raping her so selfishly.

She sobbed, "Aren't you satisfied yet? Haven't you abused me enough already, you unfeeling brute?"

He just moved in her faster, growling, "If I wasn't feeling how grand you feel in there, you pretty little thing, I wouldn't be trying so hard to satisfy us both."

She sighed and said, "Oh, well, if you can't stop, you might as well go ahead and finish." So he did, and when she added, coyly, that he could have a little more, she didn't really mind, he was tempted to just stop and leave her hanging way in the middle of the air. But although he knew most men would have said she deserved it, and likely had, the poor old gal was just suffering from the confusion of screwing sober on a no doubt proper Victorian upbringing and education. So he took his time getting them there again, and had her stark naked and spouting suggestions from French postcards before they wound up climaxing again, in a far corner, with her on top.

That turned out to be a tactical error. For she'd barely come that way before she wrenched her voluminous breast from his grinning teeth, disimpaled herself from his turgid shaft, and bolted for the back of the house to lock herself safely away, she said, later, after he'd laid her again in her four-poster.

By this time it was at least nine o'clock and even an old maid seemed able to grasp Longarm's simpler view that life was complicated enough without putting on needless airs. So once he'd gotten her to admit she'd never have started up with him to begin with if she hadn't liked it at least as much as let's say beating rugs, she relaxed in his arms and even allowed she enjoyed a good smoke, when nobody from the school board was watching.

So as they shared a cheroot in the dark he got her story out of her. It wasn't one he'd never heard before in his travels. For old Queen Victoria had surely put odd notions in a young gal's head, for a lady who must have screwed Prince Albert silly to manage that many horny princes and mighty fertile princesses.

Poor Maxine had been born into a more prim and proper family than the current skirt-chasing Prince of Wales, so it had never occurred to them, or her, that some young gents expected a free sample, or at least some warm kissing, before they proposed to even a pretty young thing with no money of her own. She'd had to go to work as a school-marm for the simple reason that her folk had more dignity than dinero, after her daddy's side lost the war. And at a time when gals who hadn't been spoken for by the advanced age of twenty were lucky to get any offers at all, she had, she confessed, held out a mite unwisely for someone grand enough to meet her family's puffed-up standards until, one day, it occurred to her she was just an old maid nobody wanted.

He patted her plump shoulder when she'd said that and assured her, "Someone must have wanted you, this way, at any rate. For should you try to tell me you commenced this evening a virgin I'm likely to say something mighty rude about your veracity."

She chuckled ruefully and admitted, "A girl has feelings and, once she gets at least a little education, she finds out how many ways there may be to satisfy them. There are instruction books on every subject, if you know where to order them by mail in plain brown wrappers."

He didn't answer. As a federal deputy he didn't think he wanted to delve into improper use of the U.S. Mails. She may have taken his silence as disbelief. Toying with the hairs below his belly button she coyly confided, "All right, I found a man willing to make a woman out of me when I was over thirty, and I'll be ever grateful. Maybe I've found a few others, since. They all had the decency to let me get a little drunk, first. I'm not sure I feel right about lying here, cold sober as well as stark naked and sinful. It makes me feel so . . . I don't know, wriggle-wormy, I guess. It never drove me so wild, inside, after a few stiff drinks with a sweet young boy who wasn't, ah, quite so stiff."

He took another drag on their communal cheroot, blew a plume into the gloom above them, and told her, "I'm happy for us both, then. For I've done it drunk and I've done it sober, and I can tell you true that sober is better if you mean to make a night of it."

She must have wanted to make something of it, for she began to take the matter in hand, even as she told him in a worried tone, "I dasn't let you spend the whole night here, Custis. Whatever would the neighbors think?"

He shrugged his bare shoulders and reached out with a hand to snub out the smoke as he replied, "They'd likely think we like to screw. That's the trouble with small-town gossip. Most of the time it's accurate, albeit a mite spiteful, in my opinion.''

Then he rolled her atop him, knowing they both liked it when she bobbed her ample hips so fine with her big fine breasts sort of smoothing out his mustache for him. As she positioned her pelvis she giggled and said, ''Well, just one more time, then. But you simply have to leave before midnight, dearest.''

He cupped her big buttocks in either palm to haul her on like a sort of warm moist sheath, assuring her, ''I'm registered at the hotel, should any nosy neighbors see fit to inquire.''

So she shuddered herself down for more, moaning, ''Oh, Jesus, bite my nipples hard, you handsomely hung brute!''

Then she stiffened atop him and he felt sort of silly as well to hear little Trisha call in through the doorway, ''Are we rid of that fresh thing yet?'' followed by, ''Oh, Maxie! What are you and that strange creature *doing* in there?'' followed by the sound of running footsteps and a screen door slamming.

Maxine, stuck for anything to say, began to move teasingly up and down atop him. He chuckled and said, ''Some kids sure ask dumb questions. Do I feel all that strange to you, right now?''

Maxine sobbed, ''Christ, no! I want every inch of you! I *need* every inch of you! Just do it, darling, and I'll explain about Trisha and me later!''

That sounded fair, albeit he didn't really need an explanation in depth as he probed the depths of the lusty and no doubt sometimes lonely schoolmarm. What he really wanted to know was whether Kate Hayward had been an even earlier bisexual lover. For that might put a different complexion entire on everything he'd been told about that dead owlhoot's sister. He'd learned to his own satisfaction, both ways, that pretty little Kate hadn't been telling him the whole truth. But a lot depended on whether he could pin her down as just a sort of wild but fairly honest sister of an outlaw or the petty thief and habitual troublemaker folk here in Gooding, mostly this lusty schoolmarm, had her down as. He knew a kindly older woman swindled by a former pupil would see things one way while a lesbian lover scorned might even make up spiteful gossip out of whole cloth. So how in thunder was he supposed to get the truth out of this confused and confusing small-town sensualist, even if he asked her whether she'd been messing with her older students, male, female or whatever? He knew she'd deny it, if only to keep her job, whether it was true or not.

Then things got even more confusing when Trisha came in again, sobbing that it wasn't fair to abandon her just because a mean old *man* had come between them. Longarm figured the best course was to let them settle it between their fool selves. So he just went on humping away as Maxine patted the linens beside them, invitingly, and replied, "Oh, for heaven's sake take off your clothes and join us, sweetie. You know Mama wouldn't want you to feel left out."

The likely less experienced and surely younger gal stamped a foot and told them they were both acting just horrid. So Longarm expected her to storm out again and couldn't wait. It made a man feel sort of silly to have a fully dressed librarian staring at him as he bounced bareass atop a less formally attired friend. But the next thing he knew he had two giggling females naked in bed with him.

He naturally tried to welcome the petite and less flushed Trisha with a warm-up grab, at least. But even though he grabbed her above the waist she sobbed, "Don't touch me! I'm not that kind of a girl!"

Maxine told him, in a less hysterical tone, "She's still a virgin, Custis. Don't worry, I know how to take care of both of you and it's something I've been dying to try!"

He muttered, "Aw, shit," under his breath and propped himself up on one elbow to grope for that cheroot he'd snubbed out with the distinct impression he'd gone to bed with a lady who shared his views on down-home slap-and-tickle. He found the unlit smoke and put the wrong end in his mouth in the confusion occasioned by the more exciting oral pleasures both gals seemed to be indulging in.

The junoesque Maxine had just told the petite Trisha she wouldn't be left out, and she'd obviously meant what she'd said, but where did that leave him?

After he'd studied on the way they were going at it an inspiring time, he decided that Trisha, on top, was in the more inviting pose whether she liked men or not. So he got rid of the soggy smoke again, assumed a position over both of them, and grabbed Trisha's trim hips to slide into her natural, which inspired her to clamp down on his shaft almost too tight for comfort as she sort of hollered down Maxine's well, "Oh, my God! You'll never believe what he's doing to me, Maxie!" Which inspired Maxine to laugh like hell and order Trisha to for God's sake keep going with her own sweet face as she, in turn, began to tickle the hell out of the two of them with her lascivious tongue.

After that both gals wanted to get really down and dirty with him and he might not have escaped with his life if somewhere in the night church bells hadn't commenced to toll and Maxine hadn't sighed, "Oh, shit, it can't be that late already!"

Back at his hotel, the same desk clerk was on duty as Longarm came in, walking sort of funny. The clerk glanced up at the wall clock, yawned, and said, "I figured you'd be back. There just ain't no action in this infernal one-horse town."

To which Longarm could only reply with a weary smile, "Oh, I don't know. It's as lively a little town as some I've passed through in my time."

Chapter 7

The next morning, after stocking up on provisions and directions, Longarm didn't find the six- or seven-mile ride out to the Hayward spread all that complicated. It was moving in the last quarter mile that got complicated. The low-slung cluster of sun-silvered board-and-baton structures sprawled beneath a newer patent windmill, all surrounded by dead-flat approaches overgrown with stirrup-deep sagebrush.

Knowing a fair hand with a plains rifle could nail a man-sized target at a quarter mile if he really put his mind to it, Longarm dismounted, tethered his buckskin cayuse to a clump of sage, and mosied in the rest of the way afoot with his Winchester cradled casually over an elbow, pausing every fifty yards or so to hail the house. By the time he was within pistol range it seemed obvious nobody was home, or that they meant to open up on him at point-blank range. He circled some to get what seemed to be the blank rear wall of a chicken coop between himself and the staring black windows of the main house. As he moved in closer he could see there were no ponies in the corral out back, and surely the hens in that rickety coop should have noticed the approach of a stranger by this time if there was even livestock left on the property.

There wasn't. Longarm established as much after a heart-stopping dash from the corner of the chicken coop and a headfirst dive through a side window, only to find the house deserted.

After a more sedate look around he strode back to where he'd left the buckskin, untethered it, and mounted up, muttering, "Well, Buck, we rode out of our way a piece for nothing worth recording for posterity or even Billy Vail. The old man cut out when he learned his only son had gone bad or, not wanting anyone at all in the family to jaw with the law about young Jimmy's recent past, both the old man and old Kate have been grabbed."

That was something to think about, not too cheerfully, as he rode on to the north across the sage flats. There'd been no signs of a struggle back there. Kate had apparently lit out on her own, back in Denver. For her sake, he hoped she was neither dead nor in too deep. A very few ladies he'd laid in his time had been really murderous bitches, and he tended to recall most of his old bedroom acquaintances fondly. More than one old gal who'd wound up fond of him had remarked that the simple fact that he really liked women, as fellow human beings, accounted for a good part of his success with the same.

The only trouble with his memories of Kate Hayward involved confusion about her brain. Her body had been just swell. But try as he might he couldn't figure what, if anything, might have been going on inside her pretty little head. He didn't have her down, for sure, as a coldhearted troublemaker or a mixed-up little bundle of sudden impulses. Neither way made more sense than the other when one studied on her odd actions down Denver way. He told his pony, "Warm natured or heart of stone, Buck, would you want to run out on a friend with a gun right after someone else had taken a mighty recent shot at you?"

The pony didn't answer. It didn't have to worry its jug head about anything but which way and how far its human master wanted to be carried. Longarm knew it was even up to him whether they ever ate or watered again. He reined his mount a mite to his right to trend toward the distant purple peaks peeking over the horizon at them. For while he'd chosen to travel light in case he met up with anything worth chasing aboard this swift cayuse, sage flats were no place to be without an extra pony packing extra water.

It wouldn't have been fair to define the Snake River Plains as true desert. But away from the big river it was named for, nobody had ever accused it of being too well watered. Neither Longarm nor anyone he knew personal had been with Lewis and Clark when they'd first forged west over the Bitterroots, of course. But some old-timers allowed, and Longarm tended to go along with them on it, that there'd been less sagebrush and a lot more grass before the white man's cows and even closer-cropping sheep had come over the Divide as well.

From time to time they passed other windmills, albeit Longarm avoided riding within hailing range when he was out to make good time. He didn't need coffee, cake and gossip half as much as he needed to get up among the better grass and water that covered most of Idaho Territory. But as they passed widely scattered homesteads he could see, even at a distance, how much more sense it made to irrigate range like this with windmill water than to pray for rain. The Snake River Plains were marginal grazing land but not at all bad for grain and truck, given the plentiful ground water to work with.

But he could see by the sage and the occasional half-wild cows they spooked as they rode on, that most of the settlers were still trying to turn this land of little rain to cattle country. Which only went to show how contrary the country folk of these United States could get. He lit a smoke, made sure the match was out before he dropped it anywhere near tinder-dry sage or even more inflammable cheat grass between the silvery green clumps, and told his mount, ''I'd write me a letter to the damned fool Interior Department if I didn't know poor John Wesley Powell hadn't worn out his one good arm writing reports on how anyone with a lick of sense would manage land out our way!''

Longarm, who read on the sly, knew the smart as well as brave old one-armed geologist had been for Christ's sake *paid* to survey new western lands for opening up, but that not even the idiots who'd hired him paid any attention to Powell's shrewd advice on where it made sense to homestead and where it didn't. So the damn-fool land office let homesteaders try to raise thirsty crops like corn in natural shortgrass country or, in this case, encouraged stock grazing on land that anyone could see was meant by Mother Nature to be irrigated potato fields. Cows could survive on sagebrush and cheat grass, at gunpoint. Sheep could get by a mite better. But this was still piss-poor range and, even as it was being overgrazed even worse, the land office was encouraging greenhorns to plow up mile after square mile of thick buffalo grass on the far side of the Divide. It was small wonder all the good cow ponies on this slope seemed to be going to outlaws. It was mighty hard country for an honest cowhand to make a living in.

He met a pair of the original inhabitants of the territory later that afternoon, as he was polishing off a late lunch of cold canned beans and tomato preserves by the side of the game trail he'd been following a spell. He was naturally hunkered on his boot heels, lighting a cheroot for dessert while his cayuse finished off its nosebag of cracked corn, when he spied the elderly couple coming his way afoot. They were dressed sort of white, or at least like ragged-ass hired help, but he could tell at a distance they were not only Indians but Digger Indians, likely Northern Paiute, because the old man was striding out ahead, hands free, save a stick about the size of a copper-badge's billy, while the old woman trudging on after him was loaded down like a mean Mexican's burro.

The old Indian out on point had spied Longarm and his

pony well before, of course, and had started to swing wide, just as naturally. But Longarm wanted some information and so he rose to his feet and waved them on in.

They had to study some on his invite. But in the end they came on over, looking less anxious than they likely felt. For the Ho, as they called themselves, had never savvied the Saltu, or Strangers, any more than the white man savvied them.

Longarm had learned not to make hasty value judgments when it came to judging anyone, and he'd long since learned some Indians could be tough for even other Indians to figure. Nobody had ever managed to explain the Digger culture to anyone, red or white, who didn't share their taste for stringy jackrabbit meat and dug-up roots and bulbs. Longarm knew the old Indian wasn't trying to be mean to his old woman and that she, in turn, figured he was acting manly by walking out ahead of her as the two of them approached a dangerous and unpredictable Saltu. A man couldn't fight so good with his hands full. A woman couldn't fight as good as a man, with or without a load on her back. So, to them, the way they were getting across the sage flats with all their meager possessions made perfect sense, even to Longarm. He'd had it explained to him by Paiute in the past.

As the elderly couple got within earshot he called out, "Hear me, I ride for the Great White Father, who tells me our people are at peace forever. I have water. I have food. I have tobacco, if you would let me share with you, my Ho brother."

The old man stared back suspiciously as he answered, "Ka, we need nothing, nothing, if only you won't hurt us. We are not evil people. We are not rich people. We only want to get to the camas fields along the Sawtooths before the good bulbs have all gone to seed."

Longarm understood, to the extent a white man with an open mind could hope to. He'd eaten camas bulbs. They weren't bad in their own insipid-sweet way. But they hardly seemed worth the ferocious wars the northwest nations had had over the right to dig or not to dig the watery things. He told the old Indian, knowing he wasn't supposed to notice the old woman, "Camas taste good in early summer before they sprout too high. I am not after the good things the spirits put in the ground for my brother's people. But I am going north, far north, into the hills beyond the Sawtooths and even the mighty Salmon River. Does my brother think his people, up that way, will think I am out to bother them?"

The old Digger frowned up at Longarm to say, sincerely enough if Longarm was any judge, "There are no Ho to worry about you, one way or the other, that far north. Hear me, I think you are a good person for a Saltu. Maybe we will take some salt and flour from you, if you can spare it. But if we do, you must promise you won't go north of the south fork of the Salmon River."

Longarm got out an extra cheroot as he replied with a puzzled frown, "I don't follow your drift, my Ho brother. If none of your people roam the Clearwater country up yonder, why should you care if I do?"

The old Indian stared wistfully at the tobacco in Longarm's hand but kept his own hands down at his sides as he replied, "I just said I thought you were a good person and you just said you rode for the Great White Father. Hear me, bad things happen up there among those dark and empty hills you call the Clearwaters. When men like you go into them and fail to come out, the blue sleeves get angry and fuss at all of us to tell them what happened."

Longarm pressed the cheroot on him, insisting, "Hear me, your people and mine are not enemies. I won't accuse you camas eaters of anything, even if I meet any where you say you never roam."

The old man took the smoke with a show of reluctance,

but let Longarm light it, casually asking what sort of Indians they might be talking about in the Clearwater country ahead.

The old man took a deep drag on the cheap but at least real tobacco, rubbed his stomach to indicate how swell he thought three-for-a-nickel smoke tasted, and said, "Nobody knows. Some say Salish, some say Sahapta, the nations you Saltu call Flatheads and Nez Percé. Others say only spirits, bad ones, live high among the gray rocks of the Clearwaters."

Longarm frowned thoughtfully and asked, "Don't the Cayuse speak the same lingo as the bands the French trappers dubbed the Nez Percé?"

The older man shrugged and said, "I know little about Horse Indians. For some reason they are as bad as your kind when it comes to riding my people down as if they were rabbits."

He stared past or sort of through Longarm to add in a small weary voice, "Worse than if we were rabbits. They don't even want to eat us. They just kill us, for practice, I think."

Longarm nodded but didn't answer. He knew more advanced speakers of the same Uto-Aztec lingo felt, or said they felt, that it just wasn't right for the Digger bands to talk and even look so much like their own proud selves. Next to asking a Cherokee if he was by any chance a Creek, there was hardly any way to make a half-assimilated Indian cloud up and rain all over everyone than to ask say, a Ute, Bannock or Shoshone if he could be even distantly related to a Digger. But, hell, the long-standing dislike of Horse Indians for Diggers, and vice versa, had little or nothing to do with the case he was on. Whether that part-Cayuse breeder, Arquette, shot Diggers on sight or not, he hadn't been accused of selling them any ponies, and so far, knock wood, no Indians of any nation had taken to pulling stickups mounted so fine.

So Longarm said he'd keep an eye out for evil spirits and bad Indians up where he was headed, and made as if to go haul his pony's muzzle out of the nosebag and be on his way. But then the old man sort of spoiled his plans by asking quietly, "Do you know if the ones who have been following you are red Saltu or white Saltu?"

Longarm cocked an eyebrow to stare past both the old man and his hunkered down old woman a few yards south as he replied, in a noncommittal tone, just in case this was some attempt at obscure Indian humor, "I can't say, at this range. How far off did you say you made 'em out?"

The Indian said, "You are staring the wrong way. It is only one rider. He is too smart to ride behind you in open country, as if he was a very young coyote."

"Where, then?" asked Longarm, knowing better than to spin around and around on one heel like a nervous nelly who'd just been told there might be mice in the house.

The old Indian said, "He was off to your southeast when I spotted both of you a little while ago. When you reined in and got down, he did the same and I lost sight of you both for a time. When we found you had stopped just off the trail we were following, it was too late to avoid both of you. I am glad it was you and not that other rider we caught up with in the sagebrush out here. If you are a lawman, as you say, then he must be an outlaw, if he is white, or looking for trouble, even for a damned Shoshone, if he is one of them."

Longarm didn't have to glance up at the sun. The shadows all around told him it was just a tad to the west of the zenith by now. He decided, "If someone's ghosting along my horizon with the sun in my eyes he'll likely work around to my west as we ride on. Unless he's just a mighty curious cuss, he's holding out for sundown and the cover of darkness before he tries anything more serious."

The old Digger nodded soberly and said, "I don't think he'll try for you in daylight, either. If you started back to town, right now, you could get there before it got dark, you know.''

Longarm nodded, but asked, ''Now why in thunder would I want to do a dumb thing like that? I'd never in this world be able to pick him out of the crowd in town and, come sunrise, we'd both be back where we started this morning. So there has to be a better way, my Ho brother.'' He stared thoughtfully to the north, adding, ''Seeing you know these sage flats better than me, let's talk about where sly old coyotes like us would set up an ambush, along about sunset, at the rate I've been riding.''

By late afternoon Longarm had to conclude that unless the old Indian had been out to green a white man, and such things happened, anyone else out to give him a hard time had to know his way around a sagebrush. For try as he might, Longarm couldn't spot the son of a bitch, and Longarm knew a thing or two about scouting in and about wide open spaces.

For openers, he knew flat and apparently coverless plains didn't have to be exactly what they looked like. The Snake River Plains were nowhere as plain as they appeared on the map, and by now Longarm was closer to the hilly highlands to the north than he was to the fool river. So the sage-covered range all around undulated like a lazy sea to begin with, and of course the stirrup-high carpet of silvery sage could hide a multitude of dry washes and other sins. Longarm knew the narrow game trail he was following, on the old Indian's advice, couldn't be seen from, say, a dozen yards off to either flank, and had it been winding up a wash that drained the purple heights ahead, he and his buckskin would be invisible to anyone just outside of pistol range.

From time to time he reined in on a rise to glance back and, when that didn't work he took to twisting in the saddle at the bottom of a gentle dip. But while he could see his own pony was stirring up a little dust in its travels, he couldn't spy any such dust against the clear horizon all about. The afternoon weather was about as nice as it ever got in these parts, so the visibility was clear and crisp beneath a cloudless cobalt sky. Up ahead, five miles or more, he could see the long low ridge the old Indian had told him he might reach before sundown. And just as the old wandering Digger had promised, there did seem to be a notch through the east-west lava flow or outcropping, and the narrow uncharted trail he was riding did seem to lead right for that easier way through the unmapped and likely rugged obstacle.

He reined in to rest his mount and consider his options. He got down to water some sagebrush while he was at it, and as he buttoned his jeans again he told the buckskin, "If there's another rider within three miles of us he's mounted on a mole."

He lit a fresh cheroot and added, "Of course, as George Armstrong Custer discovered to his chagrin in the summer of '76, you don't have to dog a man's ass like a sniffing hound if you've some idea where he might be headed. It's just as easy and sometimes smarter to circle him wide and get there ahead of him."

The pony had no suggestions to offer as Longarm led it a spell on foot. A slow stroll was just as restful as standing still, and standing still got you nowhere at all. He contemplated that low distant pass as they kept drifting toward it. It felt good to change the way the blood got to run through his legs after almost a full day in the saddle. But there was no need overdoing it and he was about to remount when he had a better notion.

He bent over to lift the buckskin's near forehoof, telling it, "I know you don't have a stone in your shoe, pard. But to anyone scouting us from yonder high ground I want it to look as if we're having trouble getting there. I don't want him wondering how come we're about to get caught by sundown out here on the more open ground. I want him to go on hugging his fool self for riding so slick if he circled to lay for us up ahead, where anyone who knows the country would expect us to be, around sundown.''

He led the pony on another furlong, mounted up, and held it to a slow walk with the reins as he made a show of whipping at his mount's rump with his battered Stetson. He made sure not to really let the hat come in contact with the buckskin hide. He was only out to confuse anyone watching. As a naturally frisky young cayuse who hadn't been run all day, the critter was confused enough by the conflicting signals to act up a mite. Longarm let it rear a couple of times. Then he put his hat back on and dismounted, smiling wolfishly as he confided to his jugheaded mount, "Bueno. Any fool can see you just don't want to carry me no farther on that hoof, you poor busteddown brute." But he led it on another three quarters of an hour, keeping one eye on the sun to their west. Then, as the long purple shadows were getting really tricky out on the flats, he tethered the pony just off the trail and unsaddled as sincerely as he ever did when bedding down for the night. He took the nosebag from its handy brass loop on the capacious McClellan. He knew that given some water and concentrated feed in the form of cracked corn, the critter could nibble cheat grass to its heart's content. Chewing cheat offered about the same distraction and about as much nutrition as chewing beeswax or spruce gum did a kid between meals. The only danger cheat grass offered livestock, as many a nester west of the Rockies had and would find out, was starving to death belly-deep in cheat.

Longarm preferred pork and beans on the trail, for himself. So he made an elaborate show of gathering dry cheat and sage roots for a fire. But he didn't light it just yet. He placed his saddle about ten feet from the pile of brush and spread his bedroll so his feet would sleep warm while his head slept cool in the crisp thin air after dark.

Then he kept puttering around until it got too dark for him to see the line where that long low ridge rose above the sage between hither and yon. He figured if he couldn't see that far now, nobody that far could see him worth mention. So he began by moving his pony, barebacked but still bridled, off to one side and around his mock campsite to the north, covering that approach along the game trail. Then he tied the reins to yet another brush and strode on back to where he'd put on such a show of setting up for the night. Working as fast as he could, since he didn't know how much time he still had to work with, Longarm plumped up his otherwise flat bedroll with sagebrush and put his hat over the "face" of his ghostly sleeper. He slid his Winchester from its saddle boot and, as long as he was at it, broke out a couple of cans for his own fool self. Then and only then he hunkered down to light the cheat-grass tinder of his camp fire, and of course he was long gone by the time the results had become a cheerful circle of flickering orange light, revealing what seemed to be his good old self, enjoying a well-deserved early bedtime after a long day in the saddle.

Nobody scouting from high ground at any distance would expect to see a pony tethered within sight of a night fire. Longarm made sure he didn't cut between said fire and that distant notch ahead as he circled around to where his pony really was. It seemed glad to see him again. But Longarm cussed when he heard it nicker to him. He said, "This'll never do, you gabby cuss," and untethered it to lead it farther off the trail. Then he not only left it way off to itself but cut back to the trail on the diagonal to make certain the damned fool pony didn't call out again, smack behind him.

When he found the trail again in the almost total darkness he hunkered down among the sage, with his Winchester across his knees, and cut open first the can of beans and then the tomato preserves for supper. He was dying for an after-supper smoke as well, but whether tobacco was bad for you or not at any time, lighting up at times like these could take years off a smoker's life.

So he was chewing a cheat grass stem, silently cussing Digger Indians in general and one in particular, when he heard not the hoofbeats he'd been listening for but the much softer crunch of boot leather on grit.

Longarm froze, nerves atingle, trying not to even breathe as he felt sure his heartbeats alone would give his position away. But they didn't seem to. The invisible other easing down the trail didn't seem to be breathing, either. But of course there was just no way to tread dusty gravel soil or brush one's legs through dry sage without making any sounds at all. So Longarm could tell the mysterious stranger was coming. He just couldn't pinpoint the son of a bitch in the dark and, even if he'd been able to draw a bead on him, it wasn't as if a lawman or even a halfway decent gent got to simply fire without the least notion of who the target might be. Hickok had blown away one of his own deputies doing that one time, and everyone sort of agreed he'd deserved to be called Wild Bill, even if his name had been James.

Longarm almost gasped in surprise when a low star winked out of a sudden and he realized how close his night caller had just passed by him. Longarm waited a few heartbeats and slowly rose to his own feet. He eased sideways until, sure enough, he had the sneak outlined against the glow of his own fake camp.

The outline was that of a man dressed cow. Longarm would have been surprised to have an Indian pussyfooting in on him in these parts after the good licking the Shoshone had taken just a short spell back. Longarm stepped out on the path to follow, his Winchester trained on the cuss from hip level. It hardly seemed likely anyone with innocent intent would dismount way out in the dark and creep in on the fire of another man riding lonesome. But unless and until the mysterious night creeper made an overtly hostile move, he rated the benefit of the doubt. Some gents were just naturally shy in country rough as this. Back-shooting a local cowhand, just checking out a stranger camping on his range, would be mighty tough to explain, and what the hell, thought Longarm, it wasn't as if it was his own fool self outlined against that orange glow, right?

Then he learned he was wrong when a hoarse voice screamed, "Harry! Behind you!" and the next few split seconds proceeded to get noisy as hell.

Longarm fired at the one he could see, on his way down, and worried less about who he might have shot when the night was rent by a fusillade of repeater rounds pegged in his general direction.

But general was not only not good enough in any gun-fight, it was downright stupid in a night action to stay in one place as one fired blind. For Longarm landed on one side as he threw himself to the dirt and then kept rolling to come back up in a spread-leg crouch and fire just once at the bouquet of muzzle flashes back that way.

He crabbed well clear of his own muzzle flash, of course, and when he cocked a cautious ear to listen for any further word on the subject, all he could hear were the night winds softly humming through the sagebrush all about.

There wasn't anything sensible he could do about the spooky way things had turned out, before the fire he'd built to the south died down and the moon got around to coming up, over to the east.

It was only a quarter-moon that night. But thanks to the thin clear air and the silvery sheen of the moonlit sage tops, Longarm was able to navigate on his hands and knees safely enough to find out how safe it might be to move about at all out here.

It took him the better part of an hour to discover he had the recent battlefield all to himself, unless one wanted to count the paint pony he found nuzzling up to his own tethered buckskin.

He didn't know where the extra mount there still had to be might have run off to. He thought at first that one of the sneaky pair might have ridden off on it. But he found them both about where he'd have expected 'em to wind up. The one he'd been tricking lay facedown on the trail, across his own Henry repeater, dressed all in blue denim and dead as a turd in a milk bucket.

The one who'd been tailing Longarm, and been dumb enough to advertise it, lay just off the trail on his back, armed and dressed about the same, but still breathing, sort of funny.

Longarm hunkered down beside him, hauled out the dying man's Starr .36 lest someone get hurt, and said cheerfully, "This part of Idaho must be higher in the sky than it looks. They tell me human brains don't work so good at high altitude, and all three of us just acted sort of stupid."

The young cuss he'd shot didn't answer, if he'd heard at all. So Longarm added, "Never mind how I should have guessed your pal down the trail might have someone covering him, and never mind how dumb it was of you to yell a warning when you had my dumb ass cold. It's my considered medical opinion, speaking only as a layman who's been in more firefights than most doctors, that you'd best tell me who I ought to get in touch with for you, unless you'd as soon moulder evermore in an unmarked plot of unhallowed ground."

The kid he'd gunned didn't answer. Longarm struck a match, moved the flame back and forth across the owl-eyed ashen face, and savvied why. He shook out the match and muttered, "Well, seeing that one pony is going to have to pack you boys double to the next town, we'd best get you lashed aboard right, before you go stiff and clumsy-riding on us."

He'd led both ponies in closer to his fake camp to begin with. He tossed some brush on the coals of his spent fire to give himself more light to work with. But he didn't notice, until he'd resaddled his buckskin and commenced to lash his possibles back on the McClellan, just how jug-headed the other pony looked.

His own mount was between it and the low fire, casting a dark shadow on any brand it might have on its piebald hide. Longarm moved the buckskin out of the way and, sure enough, the paint was branded Double Tipi, which inspired Longarm to observe, aloud, "Well, that just goes to show not even Billy Vail can always be right. Or maybe it just means we've whittled your gang's remuda down to where it can't afford to ride so particular. We'll find out once I catch up with your breeder, Gaston Arquette, just who he might have sold or bestowed you upon, Paint. Did anyone ever tell you that white blaze on your jug head looks just like a stingray fish, tail and all? If we ever meet up with another honest soul who recalls such a distinctive pony, we might just figure out what in the hell has been going on up this way."

Chapter 8

The early risers on the dusty streets of Rocky Bar, Idaho Territory, found Longarm an admirable as well as spooky rider when he showed up at dawn with two dead bodies as well as two ponies with the same brand and cayuse lines. The town law and his deputies were willing to buy Longarm's story about the shoot-out once he'd shown them his more impressive badge and I.D., but they told him to his face they didn't see how he'd ever covered the sixty-odd miles from Gooding in such a short time.

Longarm explained, "I'm in a hurry and cayuse ponies were never bred to shilly-shally. To tell the truth, packing those dead boys through the hills in the dark must have inspired both of 'em a mite. I noticed I tended to dwell on the gloomy company in the dark, when we took trail breaks."

In the end, or at least a couple of beers later at the combined saloon and general store, the local officials agreed to display the two dead boys on a north-facing cellar door as long as they didn't stink too bad, and then plant them over by the city dump if nobody at all came forward with an educated guess as to who they might or might not have been. The town marshal allowed it only seemed fair for Longarm to let them have that one paint pony. But Longarm pointed out he might need the dead outlaw's mount, or to be more accurate, its registered brand, as government evidence. He said he didn't care if they kept the outlaws' gear and even weapons, though, since they or their leader had gone out of the way to make sure they hadn't been trailing anyone with anything easy to trace back to where they might have come by it.

Once he'd gotten the early-morning chat out of the way Longarm treated himself and both ponies to four hours rest, and then fed them real oats and himself a warm meal and plenty of black coffee before he was ready to ride on again.

When the now less-suspicious town marshal pointed out that he'd left himself only half a day's riding Longarm explained, "I got more than one reason to push on hard and do some of my riding after dark. The gang I'm scouting has to know my general intent and direction. The two you just took off my hands might still be alive today if I hadn't given them such an easy crack at my slowpoke ass. So I aim to keep 'em off balance by not following any regular hours or, hell, trail. I got me a survey map showing more than one way north to Orofino in the Clearwater country."

As he mounted the buckskin, figuring the paint still had some recovering from its double load coming, the older local lawman spat thoughtfully and warned him, "Don't let that survey map lead you astray, Uncle Sam. How accurate maps get drawed depend a heap more on who drawed 'em than they might on the lay of the land."

Longarm agreed he'd seen the maps the Fremont Expedition had left to posterity and heeled on up the wagon trace he didn't have to worry about, this side of, say, Grimes Pass.

But since that was the next choke point the gang might consider, he commenced to worry about it soon enough. The country was now more normal looking for Idaho Territory and thus a lot different than the sage flats he'd shot it out on the night before. The wagon trace followed a contour line along the west slope of the north-south and

110

certainly well-named Sawtooth Range. What the Indians called the Shining and the white men had dubbed the Rocky Mountains were far from being the dotted line of uniform peaks they seemed from out on the high plains to their east. Millions and millions of years back, for some fool reason, the North American continent had buckled up from Alaska territory clean down to Panama, but not nearly as neatly as folk back East pictured.

There'd been more than a mile of softer limestone, shale, sandstone and such spread flat atop the granite basement as it heaved and wrinkled two miles or more above sea level. So all sorts of miles-thick slabs of all sorts of rock had been tilted up at all sorts of crazy angles to be carved by time and the patient mountain rains into all sorts of odd shapes. In some stretches, such as down around South Pass, you could take a covered wagon or a railroad right over the Continental Divide and hardly notice how high you were in the sky, while up here in the poorly mapped peaks of Idaho Territory, you could barely ride an hour without having a damned alp rear up to block your path, with or across the general grain of the Great Divide.

From time to time that afternoon northwest of Rocky Bar, Longarm reined in on a hairpin overlook to observe his back trail. If he was being followed now, he failed to spot anyone suspicious. But on the other hand, he hadn't spied those sons of bitches the day before, even after that old Indian had spotted at least one of 'em for him, and that had been in way more open country!

He tried to find cheer in the fact that the rough and overgrown mountain scenery worked in his own favor as well. For the wagon trace to Grimes Pass was heavily screened a good part of the way by fluttering aspens and brooding conifers, mostly lodgepole pine, growing dense if somewhat skinny on the windward slopes this route followed.

Later that same day, watering his ponies in a white-

111

water brook winding across a meadow of grass lush enough to toss with other salad greens, Longarm consulted his government survey map and decided on trending upstream instead of down when it came time to ford the north fork of the next serious white water. He soon found himself as far off the regular route as any rider might want to get. For none of the trails he picked up on the far side seemed to want to go anywhere sensible, let alone north and south. He passed the same spruce a second time, noting how low the sun seemed to have worked its fool self in the meantime, and announced to both his ponies, "That tears it. We'd best work our way back to the main wagon trace and worry about crossing the damned Payette once we get to it!"

But that was easier said than done, even with the compass from his possibles bag to compare with the infernal survey map. For none of the woodland trails they got to wind along seemed to be on the damned map to begin with, while the alternate trail the damned army engineers had down so clear on paper didn't seem to be there at all.

As the patches of sky above got sort of lavender and the gloom between the trees all about went downright purple, Longarm repressed the dumb but natural anxiety he was beginning to feel, telling himself and his ponies, in a confident tone, "Let's eat this apple one bite at a time, boys. I know it looks as if I've gotten us lost, but it ain't us I've lost. I know where *we* are. I just can't figure out where anything else might be."

It was an old saw, but always worth repeating, even when you weren't a greenhorn turned around in strange country with nightfall coming on. For in his time Longarm had found lost greenhorns, sometimes still alive, in the damndest places. The human mind had a way of taking the bit in its teeth and bolting for home, whether it knew the way home or not, rather than letting itself feel lost in the dark.

So the first sensible thing to do at such times, after facing up to the simple fact that one was stuck, for now, was to get one's fool self more calm and comfortable. He rode on until they came to a nice break in the tree canopy, where the grassy ground sloped enough to stay dry without getting steep enough to cause problems, and reined in to announce, "We had to stop some damn wheres in the dark of the damned moon, boys." Then he got down to unsaddle, rub down, and nosebag both ponies just enough to calm them, saying, "You both got grass all around juicy enough for *me* to get by on, so let's save the cracked corn for stonier campgrounds, boys."

Then he broke out a short-handled hatchet to chop some windfall for a sincere cook fire. There were limits to how many cold meals a man might want to consume on the trail, and he was pretty sure he had this neck of the woods and a lot of it all around to his own lost self.

He didn't find out he was wrong until he'd enjoyed a good meal of warm beans and ash-baked sourdough sinkers to dunk in his coffee. He'd settled for just one tin cup of Arbuckle, lest it keep him up half the night, when the night was rent by the sound of a single shot and a distant voice called out, "Hello yon camp fire! Dast I come on in, alone and peaceable of intent?"

Longarm's neck hairs had already settled, somewhat soothed by the high-pitched tone of the wistful wayfarer, but he still rolled to his feet and edged away from the light of his fire as he called back, "Come on all you like, ma'am. But I hope you savvy I'm holding you to your word about coming in lonesome, and I'd like to be able to see your hands, both of 'em, while we're sorting this unexpected pleasure out."

The gal who'd hailed him from the woods must have understood the rules a heap better than those two rascals had the night before. As she materialized in the ruddy glow of his fire, leading a burro with her left hand and

113

holding the other hand high in the universal peace sign, he could see she was some sort of breed. Her high-cheeked face and big sloe eyes read redskin. But her hair, albeit braided Minnihaha enough to go with her fringed deerskin shirt and the beadwork band of her floppy black hat, was so blond he took it for white until she came closer. She had dark blue beaded moccasins sticking out from under the ragged bottoms of her too-large bell-bottom seaman's dungarees as well. He knew Siksika, better known to his own kind as Blackfoot, didn't belong on this side of the Bitterroots. But it was none of his business why a gal with blond hair wanted to wear Siksika shoes or a hatband beaded in another style entire. Breeds tended to get confused as well as resentful about their red relations, and it wasn't a good notion to ask 'em personal questions. He'd once had a bottle busted over his head by an otherwise sweet little gal he'd asked, at a church social, whether she'd got them big brown eyes from her mammy or her pappy's side. How the hell was he supposed to know her fool granny had been Comanche?

He told this one, whatever she was, "I got plenty of coffee and tobacco and, if you're really starving, I'd be proud to break out more beans."

To which she demurely replied, "If I wasn't hungry as a bitch wolf in January I'd have passed on by with the evening breeze. For I have had my fill of white men and I ain't so sure I ever want to smile at another Flathead."

He said that sounded fair and commenced to warm up more beans as she rid her burro of its pack saddle and turned it loose to run off forever or graze all about as its heart desired. Longarm wasn't surprised. He could see she kept her burro well fed and not too heavily loaded between meals.

He could see she hadn't had much to eat of late as he watched her demolish a pint of pork and beans and a can of cold tomato preserves. It was only over coffee, with a cheroot to puff as well, that she had the grace to tell her sad but not too unusual story.

Her name, she said, was Ingrid Anderson. Despite which, as he'd already surmised, she was Salish breed from Coeur d'Alene, even farther up the Idaho panhandle than he had to go. She hadn't taken her floppy hat off so far, but he figured it was safe to assume she was part Flathead, as the more normal-looking members of the Salish nation were called.

He was glad. He wasn't as confused on that subject as some whites were. The Salish, or most of the Salish, had odd notions of beauty. They practiced the odd custom of binding the heads of their babies against their cradle boards to distort their growing skulls. A lot of whites thought it was the Salish with the backs of their skulls flat and the tops of their skulls squished up sort of pointy who qualified as Flatheads. But the Indians had it the other way around. Some Salish bands had given up the practice, or maybe never started it, and let their kids grow up with natural or "flat" skulls as the peaky domed Salish saw it. Ingrid said her Flathead mama had been part French Canuck, pretty enough for a hard-rock miner named Anderson to marry up with legal.

Her own trouble with men had started when she'd run off with yet another mining man of Lithuanian persuasion. When Longarm allowed he hadn't heard much about Lithuanians, good or bad, she explained that hadn't been the problem. When she added that he'd had a drinking problem Longarm nodded sagely and murmured, "I've walked out on a lady drunk or more in my own time. Fun is fun, but it does take the romance out of one's love life when even a pretty gal pukes in bed."

Ingrid sighed and said, "If only that was all a drunken hard-rock man could come up with to unsettle a woman's innards. But let's not have no further discussion on the subject, Custis. Once you say a man or woman is a drunk

115

it just follows as the night the day that nobody with a lick of sense wants to be around them."

He nodded soberly and then, since it seemed to be his turn he told her more about what he did for a living, where he was going, and how come, keeping it simple and leaving out the dirty parts, of course.

She grimaced at the glowing coals of the dying fire they were sharing to tell him flatly, "I doubt you'll catch many outlaws in the Clearwater country. Hardly anyone has ever lived among those deep ravines and jaggedy peaks, even back in the Shining Times. The waters run white as well as clear. There were no beaver to trap in the Shining Times. There are no beaver now. It's not good country for anything or anyone to live in, so nobody ever has."

He blew a thoughtful smoke ring and mildly asked, "What about the big mining camps like Orofino, Grangemont, Pierce and such?"

To which she replied with a snort of dismissal, "You just said your ownself they were mining camps. You find veins of gold quartz in granite country. You don't find much else. Granite don't weather to fertile soil. Snow water running over granite is just swell to drink. That's why they call it the Clearwater country. Only the water's so infernally pure that nothing much grows in it."

She began to betray her Indian heritage by talking with her hands as well as she drew pictures in the air and sort of pontificated, "Picture one big granite slab, nobody knows how thick, heaved up to start out table-flat, a couple of miles above sea level."

He nodded and said, "I can read. The geology professors describe the Clearwater country as a base-leveled, uplifted and dissected granite shield."

She wrinkled her nose and muttered, "They would. Hear me, we are talking about one big rock pile, Custis! Most of it has never been mapped. A lot of it has never been seen by human eyes, red or white. It's bad country.

No beaver, little in the way of fish or game, and even if you don't get hopelessly lost in the maze of deep canyons, they have a way of flash flooding, even on a sunny day, to sweep away anyone rash enough to dare the spirits who like to be alone with the hawk-winds that make it snow in summer on the higher peaks.''

He smiled thinly and said, ''You sure make the Clearwater country sound like a swell place to visit. Since you just said most of it's still unknown territory, I got to. But taking this apple one bite at a time, Miss Ingrid, I got to get there alive and well before I can explore for outlaws in its dimmer recesses. I told you I've brushed with would-be ambushers getting no farther than I have. If the gang knows its way *out* of the country they seem to be getting their mounts from, they must know a hundred good ambush sites between here and, say, Orofino.''

She nodded and replied cheerfully, ''More than a hundred. We're talking six or seven days on a mighty bumpy trail. Even a white boy with some sense of hide-and-go-seek could find a good spot every mile or so to lay for you with a rifle, if he knew you were coming up that particular trail.''

He nodded and said, ''So I've noticed. You met up with me out here in these confounding woods because I got turned around this afternoon trying to avoid the regular route to just the next infernal pass. But I suspect that if I had a guide who knew this territory as good or better than any bandit—''

''I don't want to lay no other man, just yet,'' she cut in, matter-of-factly.

To which he could only reply in the same clinical tone, ''Nobody said nothing about slap-and-tickle, Miss Ingrid. I need to get to Orofino in one piece a heap more than I need a piece. So hear me out before you decide one way or another.''

She shot him an arch look and sort of jeered, "That'll be the day, a week on the trail, with no chaperone."

He blew smoke out his nostrils and growled, "You sure are an insulting supper companion, considering who paid for the supper. I'll never understand what gives you womenfolk the right to assume you can have your way with us any time you please, just because one of us was nice enough to talk to you."

That shut her up a spell, since her gender was more accustomed to spouting that line than defending themselves from it. So he quickly said, "Look, we're both in a hurry and Orofino can't be much out of your way if we both ride north together. I stress the verb, *ride*, because I have an extra pony and I couldn't help noticing you got this far leading that burro afoot."

She didn't answer. He could see he had her thinking. She didn't look dumb enough to think she could walk as fast, or comfortable, as a good cayuse pony could carry her. So he just said, "Your burro can likely keep up, if we take it easy. I ain't about to gallop over many rises, blind, even with you showing me lesser-known shortcuts."

She said, "I want some more coffee, if you can spare it. I know how to get from here to Orofino and beyond to my own country without pestering any white folk about our progress. Do I get to keep the cayuse once I see you safely to the Clearwater country?"

He hesitated, nodded, and reached for the coffeepot as he told her, "That sounds only fair, provided you let me show both ponies around when I get up to their home range with 'em."

So she said she'd be proud to sneak him that far north and maybe tarry a day or so with him and the fool ponies, once they got there. As he poured her third or fourth cup of Arbuckle, brewed cow-camp strong, he pointed out she might have trouble getting to sleep with that much java in her. She took the tin cup in both hands anyway, saying,

"It's not that late, and seeing we're going to have to spend the next few nights together in any case, there's no sense in commencing our relationship with sleepy screwing, is there?"

So the pretty little breed got Longarm through any ambushes any white mastermind could have planned, by way of back-country game paths few whites had ever even guessed at. She allowed she'd have gotten them lost, herself, if here and there some long-dead Indian hadn't left a mark Longarm had trouble spotting before she pointed it out to him, and he was a cut above average when it came to finding his way in strange country.

He suspected they might have made better time along her twisty mountain pathways, had Ingrid not insisted on displaying so much of herself as part of the pretty scenery he was enjoying in the line of duty, should Billy Vail ever ask.

Not content with bedroll cuddling under the brilliant summer stars of the high country, Ingrid insisted on a refreshing dip almost every time they passed a mountain tarn, and there were a lot of such ice-water puddles along the windward slopes they mostly followed. Of course, once a poor little gal had goose-bumped herself nigh blue in snow-melt a true gent had to do his best to warm her up again, and so many a trail break turned out a mite longer than he'd have taken if he'd been traveling alone.

He found her casual approach to clocks and calendars easy enough to abide, once he got used to the notion they were really alone up among the wind-tortured trees of the higher slopes she fancied for skulking and screwing her way along.

She did both well. Despite the mean things some said about mixing her two races, Longarm had noticed and Ingrid tended to prove that the results of crossbreeding

119

could be ugly as sin or pretty as a picture, and she hadn't turned out ugly.

He suspected, from the way she ripped her duds off every chance she got, that the little half-Flathead knew her bare body displayed the best points both races had to offer. Her hair was ash-blond, all over, while her smooth tawny hide could and did take the high altitude sun without blistering as it might have if she'd been pure Scandinavian, careless as she was about basking so freely and often in the thin mountain air. Her breasts were Indian-proud if not down-right chunky. Her hips were trim and her thighs were just as solid. Yet she had the longer torso and slimmer waist-line of a white gal instead of the stubby torso that so often went with such solid breasts and derrieres. Her face wasn't bad, either, which was just as well when a gal enjoyed kissing a man, all over, as much as this one did.

Just as important, if not more so, she taught him how much his own kind owed the friendlier sorts of Indians in the winning of the West. For while he already knew a heap of woodcraft, and knew how much of it derived from handed-down Indian advice, Ingrid Anderson, like the better known Bird Woman who'd shown Lewis and Clark the way to get through these same hills back at the beginning of this same century, kept surprising him with family secrets.

She was far from the first Indian or part-Indian Longarm had ever foraged with. So he naturally knew how to tell insipidly sweet camas or flavorful mountain onions from the treacherous death camus that tended to ape either. He knew, as their canned provisions ran low, that clubbing a porcupine instead of shooting a rabbit for supper provided a tastier meal less apt to attract the attention of nosy neighbors on the far side of a ridge.

She didn't have to teach him how to stuff a trout with wild onions and bake it in a coat of clay that scaled as well as cooked the fool fish for you by the time it baked

120

hard. He knew his way in the wilderness enough to get by. What surprised and sometimes delighted him was the way she always seemed to know just where to dig for bulbs, cast a fishhook, or corner small game they could bag without gunshots.

Other times, she puzzled him by choosing, right, between two ways over a rise that looked about the same to him. Just once, to prove she might not know everything, he insisted on following the east fork after she'd decided the west fork of a narrow mountain trail might be better. It hadn't resulted in total disaster. The remote cattle spread over the next rise had been inhabited by whites too casual to pay much attention to their own baying watchdogs. So Longarm and his pretty guide had been able to crawfish back and around the outfit undetected. When he'd asked her to tell him how in thunder she'd known there were whites settled in that lonely mountain glen, if she'd never been there before, Ingrid had gone all teary eyed as she'd tried in vain to explain. For all she could come up with was that the way the peaks stood against the sky all around had made her feel it was the sort of setting white folk might choose to homestead. She allowed she didn't know why. It was just so, the way the silent spruce trees grew higher up the mountainsides than the laughing aspens. She said she didn't need reasons. She just had to know. She said her white father and red mother had argued about such silly matters when she was little. It took him a while to learn why her habits seemed so Indian, despite her name and ash-blond hair. One day her big blond daddy had simply vanished from the Coeur d'Alene country. Ingrid couldn't say whether he'd fallen down a mine shaft or simply gone on to dig somewhere else. She told Longarm she didn't see as it mattered, one way or the other, once a man was gone. For, either way, his womenfolk had to get on as best they could without him.

From time to time, on some high lookout, Longarm

would get to check where Ingrid thought they might be, now, against that government survey map. The dudes with scientific instruments to guess with had only mapped gross features, of course. But Longarm was pleasantly surprised to see how close mapped-and-measured mountain peaks agreed with little Ingrid's half-breed hunches.

As he learned not to argue with her about her Indian intuition he sensed how poor Lewis and Clark must have felt the day Bird Woman led them unerringly to her own Shoshone band, led by her own big brother and willing to sell them all the ponies they needed, after all she'd been through up until then.

Kidnapped by enemy raiders as a no doubt pretty child, the gal whose name had likely been more accurately spelled as Sakakaweeha had been sold as a sex slave and passed on from one gent to another until she'd somehow wound up the play-pretty of a French Canadian fur trader called Charbonneau, way back east at Fort Mandan. So she'd only been allowed to tag along as a pregnant afterthought when the Lewis and Clark expedition hired her drunken brute of a squaw man as a guide.

It had been a smarter move than some they'd made. Charbonneau collected Indian as well as white pornography, but didn't know how to read a map, while another French Canadian they hired to guide them over the Shining Mountains, Pierre Cruzatte by name, was later remembered mostly as a merry cuss who played a fair fiddle and shot Captain Lewis in the ass one day in the mistaken assumption he might be an elk.

Bird Woman had proven more useful, once she'd had her half-breed baby along the trail in time to lead them through the Bitterroots and beyond, all the way to the Pacific. Longarm was surprised one night as he and Ingrid shared an after-loving cheroot, to learn his latter-day wilderness guide had never heard of Bird Woman. When she asked Longarm how the story of the helpful young

122

Shoshone gal had turned out, Longarm could only sigh and say, "Rotten, considering all the credit Lewis and Clark got for finding a damned ocean everyone had always figured had to be there. The baby she bore and toted most of the way grew up white, or tried to. He might have treated his mother better than the rest of us did, had she held on until he was old enough. She died of consumption or something, some say booze, when her baby, Pomp Charbonneau, was about two or three."

She shrugged in a resigned way and observed, "If the white man's bugs don't get you his firewater will. Do you reckon the ponies Bird Woman's big brother sold her white pals were good as the two cayuse mounts we've been riding, Custis?"

He blew some smoke at the Milky Way streaking the blackness above them before he decided, "They never described the ponies they got off the Shoshone and they even called the poor folk Snakes. I doubt they'd have noticed, either way. The Indians got the horse in the sixteen hundreds, off the Spanish to the south. I doubt the Shoshone or even Cayuse were breeding riding stock before the seventeen hundreds. But, yeah, they could have had a distinct line going by the turn of the century. We'll never know for certain where the ugly but sudden cayuse originated. There are even white cow-pony breeders who don't keep stud books. As an educated guess I'd say the cayuse was a sport of nature, like the prettier Morgan pony that just appeared out of nowhere amid the remuda of a Massachusetts horse dealer called Justin Morgan, back about the time of the Battle of Bunker Hill. Nobody knows what old Justin Morgan did to deserve such an outstanding example of horseflesh. Things like that just happen now and again. I reckon Dame Nature is more democratic than folk who go by pedigree being so important for man or beast. The first cayuse pony must had happened much the same way."

Ingrid yawned and said, "I like my pinto better than any sissy-looking Morgan. I'll bet he could beat a Morgan or even a thoroughbred in a run for money. So there."

Longarm laughed lightly and said, "Let's not get carried away with Indian patriotism, honey. Nothing can beat a thoroughbred in a flat-out race over a measured course. That's how come they call 'em racehorses." Then, lest she feel he was low-rating her horse savvy he felt obliged to add, "Of course, over a rough course or chasing stock through timber any cow pony has a thoroughbred beat hollow. A cayuse combines the features of speed with the agility to turn on a dime and—"

She snuggled closer and began to grind her pelvis against his bare hip as she yawned again and observed, "I don't want to study on nothing but screwing or sleeping, being in the mood for either right now." So he put the thought aside to take her in his arms again. He knew he'd have plenty of time to wonder about ponies by the time he caught up with half those outlaw riders aboard the same.

Chapter 9

Ingrid led Longarm into Orofino, the modest metropolis of the Clearwater country, after dark as per plan. For if the first bonanza days of the brawling mining camp were commencing to fade to fond memories, the hard-rockers working for day wages were still mucking a heap of color from the slopes above the wide-open mountain town, and so naturally there were plenty of whores and gamblers to assure the redistribution of wealth the length and width of the valley.

Ingrid, who knew the country better, had told Longarm they'd just incorporated Orofino as the seat of Clearwater County, which seemed only fair when one considered nine-tenths of the local population had to be living or lurking about the only action for many a lonesome mountain mile. None of the smaller settlements up or down the three branches of the Clearwater River had enough folk dwelling in or about 'em to justify the niceties of civilization, such as libraries, banks or bordellos. But Orofino even sported a hotel across from the town livery. So Longarm checked himself in with Ingrid after they'd both unsaddled, rubbed down and saw to the burro and ponies' other needs.

Ingrid seemed more impressed by the corner room and bath than he was. In most decent hotels, by now, you got a claw-foot tub or at least a shower stall when you hired a room and bath for a whole damned dollar. All they'd given him and "Mrs. James" consisted of a corner sink and crapper. But she allowed it had crawling out of a bedroll and running for the bushes in a rainstorm beat by miles. She said she could get clean enough, where it mattered, by sort of sitting astride the sink. So he said he'd be back in no more than an hour, and added in a jovial tone that she could start without him if she just couldn't wait.

She didn't think it was funny. She followed him out in the hall, demanding to know where he was going and why she couldn't come along. He explained, "I don't want to introduce you to the county sheriff as Mrs. James, and I ain't sure who else I may run into, going or coming from the courtesy call I owe the county."

He saw he'd worried her more than he'd intended and quickly added, "I doubt any of them cayuse-riding outlaws could know I was within a week's ride of here, thanks to you and your sneaky Indian trails. But I'd still feel easier in my mind, knowing it was only my own back I had to worry about, no matter what. After I jaw some with the local law I'll see if I can scout us up some sandwiches and a bucket of beer to turn in with."

That seemed to cheer her considerable. So they kissed and parted friendly. He eased down the stairs and asked the old coot riding herd on the room keys for directions to the sheriff's office. He was told, "The county jail's ahint the courthouse, two cross streets to your left as you go out yonder door. If there's nobody there, and there might not be on such a slow weeknight, try the Pirate Saloon across from the jail. There's usually somebody there who'd know where the deputies on duty can be found, after suppertime."

Longarm thanked the old-timer and headed the way he'd been directed, scowling some. He figured there had to be close to a thousand souls in this mining, market town, and county seat, unless he'd seriously misjudged the number of lamplit windows on the way down into the valley after dark. Trail towns a lot smaller had a night shift on duty after dark, unless things were awesomely peaceable or the town law just didn't give a shit.

As he passed the open doorways of other saloons along the main business street he decided it had to be the latter. For the boys were sort of whooping it up in more than one rinky-dink establishment, and even a one-saloon town was usually good for two or three serious altercations an evening when you allowed mining men and cowhands to drink within the same city limits.

He knew the late James Butler Hickok had indulged the boys in an every-man-for-himself attitude toward peace and quiet during his short stormy career as marshal of Abilene. He'd been fired for keeping the peace in the Alamo Saloon when he wasn't dealing cards in the back room at the Metropolitan. As if to prove what a bush-league way that had been to police any town, a heavyset gent wearing chaps and the features of a pure-blood Indian reeled out of a doorway Longarm was passing to stare owl-eyed at the tall deputy and announce, "Jesus H. Christ, I really hate you white bastards, even when I'm sober, and right now I'm invincibly drunk!"

Longarm smiled agreeably, replied, "You surely have yourself a problem, Chief," and blocked the drunken Indian's roundhouse right with his left elbow to drive an amiably intended right jab into the drunk's paunch in hopes of calming him some.

It worked. Longarm kept walking as the shorter but stockier man flopped about in the dusty roadway, barking like a sea lion dying for a fish. Nobody else seemed to pay much attention, either. Then Longarm spied something more worth paying attention to. So he did. He paused by the hitch rail in front of yet another hole-in-the-wall drinkery and struck a match to study brands as he excused his nosy nature by lighting a cheroot.

Both ponies were branded Double Tipi. He hadn't needed matchlight to make sure they were both buckskins with cayuse lines. Longarm shook out the match and eased up on the plank walk. It was a free country, after all, and if gents who came to town on suspicious mounts didn't want him drinking with 'em, they could just do whatever they had a mind to about it.

But in the doorway he was frozen in his tracks by yet other considerations. For while he'd only thought the piano music coming from inside was awful, he now had a better view of the piano player down at the far end of the bar. Worse yet, the voluptuously proportioned henna-rinsed brunette in the rust-red velveteen dress was facing sideways to the door as she abused the poor piano. So he knew she only had to turn her pretty face a quarter-turn and he'd be up to his ass in a cat fight.

He crawfished back from the light, muttering to himself, "If that don't prove lady luck a lady in cahoots with all others of her gender I don't know what does!"

He knew that had he ridden into such an out-of-the-way town on his own the odds against his meeting up with his old pal, Red Robin, would have been astronomical. He knew the odds on Red Robin allowing him to sleep in peace or any other way with another gal were even wilder, and old Ingrid seemed a mite possessive as well.

He moved down the walk to keep an eye on the scene inside through the grimy glass of the saloon window. He wasn't too concerned with the great lay who played piano so badly, unless she spotted him, as he was the gents bellied up to the bar between them. For at least two of 'em had come into town aboard mighty suspicious ponies.

As he stood out there smoking and no doubt looking suspicious to anyone passing, he got the feeling from the relaxed attitude of everyone inside that except for Red Robin, it was the regular crowd. He'd noticed, since the first time they'd met down Texas way, that a piano-playing gal who played just awful and didn't put out for the boss or anyone else she didn't fancy tended to move on every now and again. She'd told him she felt popular when she managed to stay in one place a full month. Longarm knew she'd likely know the regulars in there, by name, at least. For if she'd been here in Orofino more than a few nights they'd all made a play for her by now.

But how in thunder was a man who valued his own hair and hide to approach such an amorous spitfire for information and information alone? Red Robin had informed him on an earlier occasion that a poor piano-playing gal who was particular about her playmates could wind up hard-up as hell. That was likely the reason she came at him sort of frothy-mouthed with passion every time they wound up in the same neck of the woods.

Distracted as he was by his conflicting desires for the natural blond charms of a gal he'd be parting with all too soon and the spitfire skills of the older artificial redhead, Longarm almost missed getting a good look at the two gents in there who suddenly or at least with no great ceremony crawfished back from the bar to head for the doorway just to Longarm's left. He saw they were both dressed too citified for cowhands but too cow for city slickers and that one, at least, had a gold-washed brass badge pinned to the lapel of his rusty-black frock coat.

Longarm had been looking for someone who might ride for the local sheriff's department, and he knew most town lawmen sent away for *nickel*-plated badges. But seeing they'd likely swing his way as they came out, if they were headed for the courthouse square farther up the way, and seeing how dumb it could be to call to a man or more as he stepped out into the darkness after sipping anything stronger than cider, he decided to let them stroll a ways and get their eyes used to the streetlamps before he accosted them.

They startled him instead. Neither turned his way as they came out through the batwings. They stepped off the plank walk to untether those two buckskin ponies branded Double Tipi. Then they both mounted up and rode off the other way. Longarm took a thoughtful drag on his cheroot and turned to be on his way, but he wasn't ready to shrug it off just yet. For while it stood to reason a lawman or more might purchase a good pony from a local breeder, the unexpected popularity of Double Tipi buckskins had raised some natural suspicions in his mind. So when he got to the county courthouse, dark and shuttered for the night, he saw no need to proclaim his name and business as he sort of sidled into the bigger saloon across the street. It was crowded enough at that hour for him to have some trouble finding a vacancy along the bar and when he did, nobody behind it or to either side seemed all that surprised to hear him order a plain draft. Longarm had long since learned the art of fitting into the crowd in all but the most tightly knit drinking establishments. Nobody paid much attention unless one went out of the way to start up a conversation or, contrariwise, sulked over one's drink enveloped in gloom. When a hard-rock miner to his right asked Longarm to pass the peanuts he did so with a pleasant but not too eager expression. That gave him the chance to ask the younger cowhand to his left if he wanted the bowl back. The cowhand didn't, but felt inspired to say, "I can see by the crush of your Stetson you're a High Plains rider. You just come over the Bitterroots from the Big Sky Range?"

Longarm allowed that was close enough. The kid had a lot to learn about taproom manners, but he seemed a friendly enough pup and it wasn't the task of a paid-up peace officer to tell kid cowhands to mind their own damned business. Talkative locals, dressed so cow, could be just what the doctor had ordered for a stranger in town who didn't want to appear as nosy as he was being paid to be.

Longarm had, in fact, once ridden with Captain Goodnight on the far side of the Bitterroots. So he was able to give the impression he was looking for work over here in the Clearwater country without out-and-out lying.

But the trouble with young gents who liked to gab with strangers in saloons was that they seldom seemed to know anything. Longarm suspected master criminals seldom confided in friendly windbags. When Longarm steered the conversation to horseflesh, assuming anyone who rode the Clearwater range for a living might have at least heard of the famous cayuse ponies raised by old Gus Arquette, it developed that the kid cowhand depended on the no doubt older and wiser head wrangler out at his spread, the Circle H, to issue him his mount of the day. He apparently didn't even have a regular string of his own. When Longarm cautiously mentioned the advantages of a cayuse over, say, a Spanish barb in country cut up so much by white-water creeks, the younger rider just looked blank and allowed he'd never noticed that much difference. So Longarm knew they had him riding drag and pitching hay out to the Circle H. But he never let on. Few outfits needed more than three or four top hands, which was why he'd gone to work for the Justice Department to begin with, as he'd noticed the original buckaroo breed of the long drives giving way to the glorified chore boy in a big hat and chaps. Longarm was sorry he'd started up with this one, now. Not because he looked down on the poor young cuss, somebody had to dig fenceposts, but because he was wasting his time with a local who didn't know beans about local conditions.

There was no way short of outright rudeness to shut the kid up as he prated on about chasing cows up or down canyons. The kid had introduced himself as Happy Blake, which figured, and so Longarm had just said they'd called him Stretch along the Goodnight Trail, which was true enough when one studied on the time he'd been over yonder working undercover, when an older and meaner looking individual bulled in to join them, rude as hell but backed by a tin star on his vest and a thoughtful hand perched on the grips of his low-slung Patterson Conversion. He was staring straight at Longarm as he asked young Happy, instead, "Might this tall drink of water be anyone we know, Mr. Blake?"

To which the well-named Happy Blake responded cheerfully, "Sure we know him. Leastways, I do. Stretch, say howdy to Marshal Rudge, Orofino's answer to Wild Bill Hickok."

Longarm put out a friendly hand. The town law ignored it to look him over from head and toe, muttering, "Well, lots of riders wear blue denim outfits and there's no law against standing tall ahint a mustache. You say they calls you Stretch?"

Longarm nodded and was about to toss in his full name when they were joined by another sinister-looking local, this one with his gun half drawn as he growled, "Is that him, Marshal?"

To which Rudge replied, "We're still working on it. Happy, here, says he knows this old boy."

The young cowhand nodded and chimed in, "Stretch and me used to ride the Big Sky Range, over on the far side of the Bitterroots. Can't you see we both got our hats squashed down to foil the damned old wind you buck on such wide-open range? You boys here in Idaho ain't never felt real wind in your fool faces and that's a fact, no offense."

The two local lawmen exchanged annoyed glances. The one who'd first spotted Longarm and come over to comment on his appearance said, "Well, like I said, a lot of riders look much the same to folk as they pass by, and it's not as if we've checked out every stranger in every saloon in town."

Longarm was tempted to quit while he was ahead. But even as they started to turn away he had to ask, "Would you boys mind telling me who you're after, seeing as the cuss may bear a possible and thus disturbing likeness to my own fool self?"

Marshal Rudge didn't answer. But his deputy, despite his ruder approach, was polite enough to answer, "Just a troublesome gent who, as you just surmised, answers to about the same description, pancake hat and all. He may answer to the handle *Longarm*. Don't mess with him if you meet anyone who fits our shoot-on-sight orders. He's armed, dangerous, and then some, the pesty son of a bitch!''

If survival had been his only consideration, Longarm would have simply forked himself aboard the first unguarded mount he'd been able to find and lit out for his life. For the odds against one man in a remote community where the law was in cahoots with the outlaw gang he was after seemed just a mite intolerable.

But they got worse when he had to consider at least two female pals who could be in danger as well. He knew neither sweet-screwing Ingrid nor rollicking-rumped Red Robin would have brains enough to call him a pestiferous son of a bitch if anyone mentioned his name in vain in front of either, as they were almost certain to if they were serious about this revolting development.

First things coming first, he scouted the hole where he'd left little Ingrid, saw they didn't seem to have it staked, and carried the beer and sandwiches he'd promised up to their hired room.

He wasn't surprised to find Ingrid stark naked atop the bedding, and he had to allow she looked mighty tempting in the coal-oil glow of the one bed lamp. But he hung his hat on the bedpost and left his six-gun on as he sat on the bed with her, handing her goodies from the big brown paper bag he'd filled just down the street as he brought her up to date, tersely, and added, "We got to get you on your way to Coeur d'Alene pronto, before they think to stake out the damned livery across the way. Lord knows who wired 'em I was coming. The nice part is that they couldn't

133

know I was heading this way so sly with a pretty little Flathead gal. I know you fancy that paint cayuse, Ingrid. But I'd be obliged if you'd settle for the buckskin I began with. The rascal who warned them I was coming described my undercover riding outfit, and no doubt put me on a buckskin mount, so—''

''What difference does it make, if we're lighting out together?'' she cut in, before biting into her ham on rye with a natural appetite a man just had to admire.

He told her wistfully, ''I can't go on with you, kitten. It ain't that I don't want to. I'm sure there's some positions we've yet to try, if only we had more time and imagination. But she travels safer who travels fast, alone, and I got enough on my plate without having to worry about your sweet hide.''

She looked as if she was trying not to cry as she washed a mouthful down with beer, belched delicately, and protested, ''I wish you'd pay attention to your loving mama, Custis Long! If we both get it on up the road you won't have to worry about either of us getting ventilated! You can't take on a whole town all by yourself. That mastermind your boss sent you after has somehow managed to buy off the law as well as the best horseflesh in Clearwater country! Your only hope is to get away from the rascals and come back here to deal with 'em, right, at the head of an army column!''

He nodded, but said, ''I have to nail down just a few more facts, kitten. Even with a troop of cavalry backing my play, I can't just arrest everyone in Orofino. There must be over a thousand souls in this valley, and it only stands to reason *some* of them are innocent.''

He helped himself to a sandwich and confided, ''I got to ask a few innocent questions as I was picking up this stuff at the Dutchman's down the way. I know which trail to follow out to Gaston Arquette's Double Tipi spread. Him and his line of cayuse mounts are well known here in

134

town, and if I didn't have cause to know better I'd be tempted to guess the local lawmen just ride Arquette stock because it's so good.''

He washed down some ham and cheese with the beer bucket, put it back on the mattress between them, and added, ''Suffice it to say, Arquette's spread is an easy ride up into the hills from here, yet well outside the city limits. I have to look for a crossroads general store cum post office and then—''

''You damned fool!'' she cut in. ''Can't you see they'll have that old breed's stud operation staked out? They know you're out to backtrack those buckskins back to where all those outlaws got them and—''

''I doubt it's that simple,'' he cut in, himself. ''One of the things that has me puzzled most, in fact, is how come they've worked so hard to keep me from getting up here to do what. I mean, they have to know we know that gang favors cayuse ponies sporting the registered brand of a well-known breeder.''

She asked, trying to be helpful, ''Won't you be able to guess who the mastermind behind all them stickups might be once you find out who bought a whole mess of matching ponies off the same breeder?''

He grimaced and said, ''One of 'em, at least, came after me aboard a black and white paint. I don't know what that means. I don't know what any of it means. For you're right, it's almost as if they were trying to get me up here, alone, to begin with.''

She polished off the last of her modest but rock-solid snack and agreed the gang had to be up to something mighty vile. Then she lay back and added with a wistful little sigh, ''Speaking of getting vile, this figures to be about the last chance we'll ever have, and I'm commencing to feel hard-up already!''

He picked up the wrappings and beer bucket and got them safely out of the way as she coyly slipped a pillow under her own trim naked hips. He knew he was going to regret this before the night was over, unless Red Robin had changed considerably since the last time they'd been in the same town together. But at the same time he knew how much easier, and quicker, it could be to just go on and do it, versus the time and trouble it could take to convince a naked lady panting with passion that you just weren't that sort of a boy.

He left the lamp lit to inspire them both, and because he was both a mite jaded with the tawny blond and looking to save some energy for the paler skinned natural brunette cum redhead he hoped to have breakfast with, he put more skill than passion into his last pleasant ride down lovers' lane with Ingrid. She naturally took his protracted organ grinding as pure flattery, and it drove her so wild that whether Red Robin still liked him or not he began to respond in kind. But just as he was working himself up to a serious bucking contest the little gal suddenly went limp under him, sobbing for mercy and begging him to forgive her for not being able to keep with him on a full stomach and worried mind. She sighed and said, "I keep expecting someone to come busting in on us, guns blazing, and to tell the truth that sounds more painful than romantic!"

He started to assure her that the local lawmen wouldn't be canvassing the saloons around town if they had any notion where he might be staying in town. Then he wondered why anyone with a lick of sense and another gal lined up would want to say a dumb thing like that. So he kissed her instead, and murmured, "Parting is such sweet sorrow, but when you're right you're right, and the sooner we send you on your way the longer you figure to live, you smart little gal."

She didn't argue about that, then. But a few minutes later, as he was helping her saddle the buckskin across the way, the old night man at the livery being too drunk to notice, she told him she felt like a rat deserting a sinking ship and begged him once again to ride out with her, saying, "I know the county law up home is honest. More honest than the sons of bitches around here, leastways. If you was to come home with me and just show your federal badge to the boys—"

"I've already considered that," he cut in. "Coeur d'Alene is just too far, no offense. If it was any closer I'd still have a time recruiting a posse unless and until I could say for sure who we were after, on what charge."

She protested, "That ain't no mystery, Custis. The very men charged with keeping law and order here in Orofino are out to do you dirty, knowing you by name as an even more famous lawman!"

He grimaced and said, "I noticed. I just hate these jurisdictional disputes. Let's get this critter and your burro outside and I'll be able to help you mount up without cracking your pretty head open."

She waited until they were out on the dark street again before she asked what he'd meant by a jurisdictional whatever. He hauled her in for a fond farewell, saying, "Just talking to myself, sardonic. I have had arguments with lawmen riding for other outfits as to just who might or might not be authorized to arrest whom on what charge. But I've seldom hit a town where the so-called law was out-and-out out to take me dead or alive."

Then he kissed her and added, "Let's get your sweet ass in the saddle, honey. I gotta find out what the boys around here are trying to hide from the outside world, and I can't hardly do that and guard your sweet hide at the same time."

But she clung to him like a lost child, sobbing, "Custis, I don't want to go. What if we never see each other no more?"

He removed her floppy hat to kiss her upturned teary face right and soothed, "Hell, sooner or later Billy Vail sends me everywhere, and Coeur d'Alene is on the same continent as Denver, ain't it? One thing's for sure, girl. We won't never see much of one another again if we get our fool selves killed here in Orofino, hear?''

Then he put her hat back on her, grabbed her sweet hips, and sort of goosed her aboard the buckskin. He spun on one heel and walked away, not looking back, as she sobbed something after him and then whipped her mount with the rein ends to ride the other way, leading her pack burro off to the north in the darkness as Longarm strode toward the brighter lights the other way.

He pondered on his own appearance as he approached that saloon Red Robin seemed to be working. Changing from his usual tobacco-brown outfit to more casual blue denim hadn't fooled anyone after all if the rascals up this way had been wired his new description, and he couldn't come up with any other way that worked. But maybe he could change the crush of his hat and shift his .44-40 to the other hip in a half-assed attempt to look more usual.

He decided not to. For he'd already been spotted and apparently passed muster as a vouched-for cowhand who just happened to answer the general description of the infamous Longarm, whatever in thunder *he* could be charged with.

He was glad he'd elected to quit while he was ahead when he got to that bitty saloon. For as he strode in he locked eyes with one of the deputies he'd bumped into before in that other place. The local who knew him on sight was at the bar, near the door, with two other sneaky sons of bitches with badges. When one stared sort of slack jawed at him the one he'd been introduced to as Stretch muttered, ''I know. But Rudge already checked him out. He's a Montana rider who just signed on with the Circle H.''

Longarm felt no call to argue that point with anyone. He moved on down the bar. The upright piano in the back corner looked mighty lonesome without Red Robin's flashy skirts spread upon its skinny black bench. He assumed she was out back enjoying a crap, or maybe just letting the boys enjoy a few minutes of restful silence. So he wedged himself in by the back corner of the bar, ordered a needled beer, and waited a spell before he casually asked if the entertainment had ended for the evening.

The barkeep nodded, just as casually, and confided, "I told Miss Robin she could knock off early. She seemed upset about something this evening, and to tell the truth she don't play so hot when she's in a *merry* mood."

Longarm sipped his drink as if it didn't matter, even as he quietly growled down into the schooner, "Wouldn't you know it. How do the contrary critters always seem to know you're after 'em?" Then he waited a spell before asking if the friendly barkeep might know where Red Robin might be staying in town. The barkeep stared at him less friendly than before as he no doubt told a big fib. But there was no way to get the gal's present whereabouts out of the old pro, even by calling him a liar. So Longarm could only smile in a sort of philosophical way. For had he not been such a horny hog about it all he wouldn't have wound up alone, entire, for the rest of the infernal night!

Chapter 10

Seeing the night man at the livery was too drunk to notice, and seeing there was no pressing reason for anyone to take his pants off now, Longarm slipped his possibles out of the hotel, leaving the hired key on the rumpled bed for the management to find after the regular checkout time, and checked himself, uninvited, into the hayloft above the paint pony he still had left to worry about.

The night passed uneventfully, save hay mites and such crawling around in his duds but not biting, and when a neighborhood rooster woke him up for good in the wee small hours, Longarm lay still a time to make sure it was safe to do so before he slipped down the ladder, loaded everything aboard the paint cayuse, and led it out front to mount up without disturbing the old drunk adoze by the doorway.

The trail they'd told him to follow out to the Arquette spread ran alongside a white-water creek on the skimpy floor of a steep-walled mountain glen. As the light got better it was still hard to say whether flash flooding or the hand of man was most responsible for the strip of grass to either side. The stock of man had surely cropped the grass short enough to play golf on. But thanks to the high water table and cool mountain climate the grass stayed emerald green, short as it had been grazed. The slopes rose a more fluttery shade of silvery green as the second-growth aspen shivered like wet spaniel pups in the faintest morning breezes. Here and there big black stumps showed between the smooth pale skinny aspen trunks, as if to explain where the more useful timber in these parts had gone. You never saw much worthwhile timber within easy hauling of a mining town. But aspen was a weed tree that sprouted on old burns or other barrens left in the wake of disasters, natural or manmade. It took him a mite longer—he had to wave a couple of scrub cows out of his way and into the aspen—before he decided what was depressing to him about a bright sunny morning ride through well-watered range.

There wasn't enough of it laid halfway flat. At first glance the Clearwater country was a lot like the so-called parklands of the Colorado high country. But the flat bottomlands between the steep ridges of the Rockies, throughout most of their length, were one hell of a lot wider and, even so, the high country didn't support the vast herds of the grasslands east of the Great Divide. Mountain meadows were far prettier, and such grass as grew there grew green and lush all summer. But there just wasn't as much of it and, in truth, it didn't seem to stick to the ribs of stock as well as summer-cured shortgrass seemed to. So mountain herds tended to be small and scattered, even where the range was laid out more sensible. Longarm could see anyone trying to graze as many as a hundred head in any of these stringbean valleys up this way would have one hell of a heap of riding to do come roundup time.

The creek he'd been following was joined by yet another, and since skinny trails ran alongside each, the results were a sort of junction with a triangular or flatiron structure of heavier logs than one could find around here, built to sort of face both trails as it narrowed to an impractical point. They'd told him in town it would. So he assumed, before he'd ridden close enough to make out the faded lettering above the plank porch, that the place had to be Garfield's General Store and Post Office, dumb as it seemed built and situated.

He tethered the paint out front, or at least on the leg of the triangle he figured he ought to, and ticked his hat brim at the old lady who stepped out the screen door with a broom in her hand and a suspicious look on her face. He said, "Morning, ma'am. I am in the market for some cheroots to smoke and maybe some coffee to brew me later, if you stock Arbuckle."

She looked a mite less disgusted and allowed she naturally stocked both. So he followed her in and waited until he was paying for his modest purchases before he casually asked if the road out front would really carry him up the creek to the Double Tipi.

That seemed to wake up the old gent in bib overalls, dozing on his heels in a darker corner, despite the early hour and crisp morning air. He piped up, "You won't find nobody there these days, young feller. Didn't you know they'd run that old half-breed out?"

Longarm kept his own voice light as he replied casually, "Do tell. That's one on me. I asked in town where the cow pony I just come by might have been bred, seeing it's branded so distinct as well as local. They told me I could likely buy a mate to it off some old breed called Gaston something or other, and that I'd find him on up this very way, but—"

"You won't," the old lady cut in. "The old fool's name was Arquette, Gaston Arquette, even though he was no more than a moon-faced Shoshone, Cayuse or whatever."

The old man yawned, scratched his belly, and said, "He might have been part French, like he claimed. Either way, he never did seem to savvy that Idaho Territory just has to collect *some* danged land taxes if it's to have any government at all."

Longarm nodded in sudden understanding. He asked, "Assuming the Double Tipi was seized for unpaid taxes, could you folk tell me who might be running it now?"

The two old hill folk stared blankly at one another. Then

the old man decided, "hell, son, nobody's been running nothing since Ferocious Ferris burnt the stubborn old cuss out, oh, a year or more ago, was it, Mother?"

The old lady, who couldn't have been his mother but might have been his wife said, "One year come fall roundup. Deputy Ferris was decent enough to give the old breed time to sell off some ponies at the best time of the year, in hopes he'd see fit to pay his back taxes. But of course he never, so Deputy Ferris only done what was right."

Longarm picked up his package with a dubious smile, asking, "Does this Ferocious Ferris always settle tax disputes with arson, ma'am?"

To which she replied in a sort of smug tone, "Only when danged foreigners defy the law of the land. I just told you they gave that cantankerous old hermit plenty of time to pay his just taxes, the same as all the rest of us. But he said he'd been there afore the Territory of Idaho and so, when they saw they could neither get him to pay his infernal taxes or get off the land, they done what they just had to."

The old man in the corner cackled self-righteously and said, "They burned down his cabin, barn, even his chicken coop and crapper. Some of his stock got burnt, too. You know how horses are about running back into a burning barn."

Longarm grimaced and said, "I've fought a stable fire or more in my time. Had I been in charge I reckon I'd have made sure all the stock was out before I played with any matches. What happened to the poor delinquent taxpayer himself?"

Again the two older folk stared blankly. Then the old man decided, "He must have just gone off somewhere. Nobody hereabouts ever saw him no more. Some of his stock was sold off by the county to pay off his just debts. He owed us for close to sixty dollars' worth of provisions. But we come out all right, in the end. Ferocious treated us decent. Took our word on how much the old deadbeat breed owed us. It do pay to elect county officials as know who's honest and who ain't.''

Longarm said he felt sure everyone in the tight-knit mountain community stuck together tight as ticks, and made as if to go. The old man got up, stretched, and asked if Longarm was up to carrying a couple of misdirected letters to the post office in town for them.

Longarm smiled as sincerely as he could manage, but told them he might not be heading into town for a spell. He saw they seemed to find his words mighty mysterious. So he explained, ''I thought as long as I've come this far, I might as well ride on to the Double Tipi and have me a look-see around.''

The old man protested, ''There's nothing there these days.''

The old woman chimed in with, ''You'd best get permission from the law afore you go poking about condemned and county-seized property, mister. Ferocious Ferris dwells just up the other fork, say three quarters of a mile. If we was you, we'd ask her permit afore we went poking up the other fork, hear?''

He smiled thinly, started to say nobody needed permission to ride up any obvious public thoroughfare, then he frowned thoughtfully and asked, ''Did you say *her* permission, as if your ferocious Deputy Ferris might be of the female persuasion, for Pete's sake?''

They both nodded. The old man explained, ''It was her husband, Ferocious Fred, they gave the badge to begin with. But when his widow, Ferocious Fran, tracked down the cow thieves who'd back-shot her man, and gut-shot them both in return, it seemed only fair to let her keep his badge.''

The old woman added, in a tone of triumph, ''She's turned out a better lawman than her man ever was, and they never called him Ferocious Fred for being a sissy. Nobody messes with Ferocious Fran in these parts. So you'd best make sure it's jake with her afore you go poking about property Ferocious Fran burnt out, personal!"

The old man, as if inspired to defend his own gender, cackled at her, "Now, Mother, you know she had half the boys in the valley riding posse with her. It ain't as if she's ten feet tall."

The old woman insisted the woman she so admired was at least as big and ten times as tough as Calamity Jane. At which point Longarm left them to fight it out and just rode on up the left fork, any interest he might have had in a backwoods female deputy sheriff subsiding as he digested the comparison with his old drinking buddy, Miss Martha Jane Cannary, the only woman ever served in Russell's Saloon in Deadwood. It had taken Russell some time to notice she was a woman.

Behind him, watching from the porch as he rode on despite their warning, the old woman told her old man, "You'd best ride up the right fork and tell Ferocious Fran, Father."

To which he replied, with a yawn, "How come, Mother? Do I look like a deputy's deputy?"

She shook her head to tell him, "You don't look like much of anything no more, you lazy old fool. But that young gent heading for the abandoned Arquette place looks just as they described that gunslick they've been expecting, blue denims, cross-draw and even that Colorado crush to his dark Stetson!"

Longarm doubted even the oddly sinister sheriff's department of Clearwater County burned settlers out on a regular basis. So when he came upon the charred remains of a smaller layout than he'd ever expected, about three miles up the narrow vale from the general store, he reined in for a look around.

There wasn't much to see. It seemed obvious enough that human habitations this far out of town lay few and far

146

between, because even a hardscrabble homestead needed at least a quarter section of reasonably flat land to drill crops into. Stock raising spreads naturally needed more, a lot more. Say a full section surrounded by enough open range to carry a herd of even modest size. So, with the creek and trail taking up about a quarter of the width of the valley floor, and the slopes to either side too steep for any critter but a goat to graze, old Arquette's stud farm, or what was left of it, had to run like a skinny green ribbon, both ways, way out of sight of the ruins that had likely stood somewhere around the middle of his claim.

Longarm dismounted and tethered the paint to a sapling near the side of the trail. The grass, ungrazed since the fire, had grown up rank, and Longarm knew such a tangle could hide all sorts of nasty junk for a pony to lame itself with. He watched his own step as he eased in on his old army boots. Where the one-room cabin had stood there was now little more to see than the stone chimney the old man had obviously invested some sweat in. The nearby barn had left more charcoal and of course some charred bones among the weedy grass stems. As far as Longarm could tell, they all seemed pony bones. He was just as glad. Now that things were shaping up this way, odd as they were, he felt safe feeling sorry for the old lonesome pony breeder. Knowing that whatever Gaston Arquette had been up to here, he couldn't have been running much of a remount station for any gang. The robberies had only started this side of the old loner's rude eviction. Some of the cayuse ponies one could sort of picture grazing up and down this long skinny valley had no doubt escaped the fire or even the roundup afterwards. The old man could have gotten away with the dozen-odd ponies one mounted man could herd somewhere, if he was good and his own mount was even better.

It worked as well, albeit not for the law, if one assumed the poor old breeder had just gone off a broken man, and that his stock had been rounded up, then sold off to justify back taxes and unpaid bills, by *whom*?

As he strode on over to the frothy stream forming a sort of back wall to the skinny property, Longarm muttered aloud, "Damned if this ain't shaping up to be one of Billy Vail's infernal paper trails after all. Nobody around here figures to tell us, even if they know, who might have gathered a choice remuda of buckskin ponies, whether here or at the county auction. But what else works?"

He stopped at the edge of the narrow but brawling white water and kicked an experimental clump of weeds in to see what might happen. The swift current whipped the clump under its foaming surface and that seemed to be that. Ingrid had said the fishing wasn't much up this way. He could see why. There wasn't a riffle up or downstream that offered a place for even a spawning salmon to pause and gather its dim thoughts.

More important than how good the fishing might have been in old Gaston Arquette's interlude as a brookside squatter, the frothy current and the almost vertical slope on the far side agreed few if any ponies, even cayuse ponies, would have run off that way the night the aptly dubbed Ferocious Fran Ferris and her posse had treated the old loner so disgusting.

He was fair minded enough to assume the night riders hadn't been out to burn any ponies to death, if only because dead ponies weren't worth beans with even their hides unfit for further use. It was a simple fact of nature that ponies spooked by smoke, flame and the noise that usually went with it tended to bolt back into a burning barn or stable, not because they had moth brains, exactly, but because their pony brains, when panicky, led them to surmise the best place to hide from all this confusion had to be their own familiar stalls. It seemed doubtful any unbroken mounts the old man had been holding for sale out here would have gone up in smoke with the rest of his property. He'd have had most of his ranging loose out here, half broke at best and—

"There he is!" a distant voice cut loose, breaking in on Longarm's thought chain and possessing him to duck, just in time, as a bullet beat its own report through the empty space he'd been about to step through. He didn't really need to hear a female banshee shout of "Get him! Don't let him get away!" to inspire his next smart moves.

There were only so many moves a man could make when he spied a dozen riders coming at him stirrup-to-stirrup, pegging pistol shots his way as they came. So for openers he took a flying broad jump at the far bank of the roaring creek and, when that didn't quite work, he just splashed across the rest of the way through the freezing armpit-deep water, scrambled up the far bank, and to hell with how steep and slick it wanted to be, and dove head-first into the screen of aspen trunks across the way.

He knew better than to stay put, of course. Even as he fought his way up the steep slope on hands and knees a fusillade of hot lead tore toothpick showers from the first patch of second-growth he'd bulled through down there. He had to grab other skinny trunks to haul himself on up the infernally steep grade, and while aspens quivered a heap for no reason at all, they did so more when a gent as big as Longarm was ape-swinging up a mountain with 'em. So that same mean voice called out, "Higher! Aim just below them treetops the big moose is shaking at you, boys!"

Longarm could hear just as well as they could. So he slid back down a piece and crabbed sideways on his rump, hauling out his own gun as the homicidal sons of bitches showered him with black mud, splinters and fluttering leaves with their ominously close albeit blind shooting. He could only hope he hadn't clogged the muzzle of his .44-40 with anything serious during his soggy escape. There just wasn't time to field strip a six-gun right now.

He held the gun in his left hand, figuring he could best get along without that if he just had to, and let them have, or at least listen to, five rounds of return fire. He was pleasantly surprised to see it hadn't done him any damage and, whether it had done anyone else a lick of harm or not, he could tell they'd stopped pegging blind shots up the slope his way. It didn't matter all that much whether they'd ducked or just paused to reload. He started climbing the mountain on the seat of his soggy jeans, reloading as he shoved himself ever higher with his dug-in boot heels. For that female posse leader was too smart by half, and if she wanted to nail him with a blind shot he sure didn't mean to rustle one damned aspen leaf to help her find the range!

After a time he heard hoofbeats. Peer as he might through the greenery between himself and the rest of the world, Longarm couldn't say, for certain, whether some of them were riding for help or whether said infernal help was arriving. He couldn't even tell how far up he might be now. But he suspected from ominous crashing and thrashing down below that some of the rascals were in hot pursuit up the sapling-covered and now even steeper slope.

He resisted the impulse to pepper them some more blind. Even if he'd wanted that slick leader guessing where he just might be right now, he had a supply problem neither she nor her infernal followers had to worry about. He'd been forced to leave behind his saddle, saddle gun and other possibles, aboard that paint pony the bastards no doubt meant to auction off right after his demise. So he had to conserve the ammunition, matches and such he had on him and, if only he could get out of this fix alive, it might be mighty interesting to see just how the county handled the disposal of a federal lawman's property.

He knew they knew he was a U.S. deputy, despite their oddly surly attitude, for he'd heard that one sullen son of a bitch mention his name in a not at all friendly manner.

But did they really think they could get away with

anything as raw as this? It was one thing to outfit outlaws with a remuda seized at gunpoint from an old eccentric breed. It was another thing entire to cover up, or try to cover up, by laying for one or more of the outside lawmen they'd been warned about by that mastermind or master half-wit.

Longarm didn't think he was immortal. He'd come too close to dying, more than once. But he knew that even if they killed him, Billy Vail and Uncle Sam would just send in others, as many others as it took, until the sons of bitches were brought to justice.

Meanwhile, they didn't seem to know that. So if it was all the same to all concerned, Longarm aimed to stay alive whether they aimed to let him or not. For he was damned if he was about to die with so many questions begging for answers in his now really mixed-up mind!

By late afternoon Longarm had gotten to know the Clearwater country a heap better than he'd ever thought he'd need to. For the leader of that posse hunting him, whether Ferocious Fran Ferris herself, or someone ranking higher in the local sheriff's department, was damned good, if a corrupt peace officer could be described as anything but bad. For every time he thought he'd lost them and tried to double back he spied some son of a bitch perched on a rock with a rifle covering that way back to town.

Longarm knew, and he knew they knew he knew, there weren't any other towns endowed with telegraph connections to the outside world within fifty miles as the crow might fly. Earlier in the day, before he'd missed lunch, Longarm had considered trying for Grangeville to the south, living off the country. But unlike the fertile high country he'd wound his way through on his way up here, the Clearwater country itself offered next to nothing to live on and promised to get cold as a banker's heart come sundown. For even the bottoms of the ravines cutting through the higher granite ridges in a bewildering maze were way the hell above sea level, and he was even higher at the moment.

For he'd been backed up a damned old sawtooth through no fault and certainly no plan of his own. He'd started out by trying to gain some time and distance on the yahoos calling back and forth through the timber all about by chasing his own shadow up a more open but still partly tree-screened slope, until he'd ducked between a pair of massive boulders to find nothing but jumbled bare granite ahead.

About that time some asshole behind him had fired a pistol shot at the sky for attention and called out, too close for comfort, "I got me some sign over here!"

So Longarm had just kept going, sudden, and whether that asshole now hopefully way back down the slope had cut his trail or not, nobody had followed him along the open winding ridgeway to the sort of flat albeit boulder-strewn top.

He doubted anyone would, this side of sundown. From up here he had a grand panoramic view across the surprisingly uniform ridges of the canyon-cut maze. The sun, now mighty low to the west, had filled the deep slots all around with almost inky shadows, but anyone moving up at him across all that bare granite, flooded by the orange glow of the gloaming, would stand out like a bedbug crawling across a clean sheet with the bedlamp lit.

The only trouble was, he knew, that he didn't dare face the night winds up here in his thin denims alone. Camping ten or twelve thousand feet in the sky could freeze one stiff enough inside a tent, under blankets, if the wind decided to blow worth mention.

He knew that once he was back down among the trees, after dark, he could keep himself this side of freezing just by walking steady, and he wasn't about to bed down anywhere before he made sure he'd shaken all those crooked lawmen out to do him dirt!

With luck they'd bed down themselves, giving him an overnight lead on them. For aside from the natural nervousness anyone might feel moving in on an armed man with a rep in total darkness, none of the bastards could want to catch up with him quite as much as he wanted to get away.

Knowing better than to backtrack down the open slopes he'd just come up, Longarm eased through the jumbled boulders atop the ridge to see how things looked down the far side.

They looked sort of grim. He thought, until he eased closer to the edge, that the sawtooth dropped off sheer to the east. But he decided a damned fool could ease his ass down, given some light or, better yet, a *lot* of light.

He gazed eastward at the purple skyline above the sunset-gilded ridges over that way. The moon wouldn't rise before the sun had sunk entire, this time of the month. But that surely was one hell of a bright star winking over the horizon at him for this time of the evening, wasn't it?

Then he knew what it had to be. Some rascal with a spyglass or scoped rifle was peering across, blissfully unaware the sunset reflecting off his lens was giving his position away.

Longarm was tempted to make a rude gesture. But that would have been mighty dumb as well as only mildly satisfying.

They probably had some way to signal back and forth. If that scout in the sky across the way had spotted him, he'd already done so. Just in case he hadn't, Longarm slowly eased himself down behind a boulder. He knew that from the other one's line of sight the height he was on would be an inky black mass against the sunset's glare. But that didn't mean he could stay up here after sundown, even if nobody else knew where he was. They wouldn't have to catch up with him and do him in if he was kind enough to freeze his own ass off for 'em.

He caught himself starting to drift a tad closer to the edge, as if to get cracking. He warned himself, "Don't you move a hair before it's dark. It's always worth hoping they don't know you're up here and, if you move about careless before moonrise, you just may get on down faster than anyone would want!"

Once the sun finished setting, the wan crescent moon took its own sweet time getting high enough to matter. In the interval of downright dangerous darkness between sunset and moonrise Longarm had worked his way well down the slope to his south, knowing that while they'd likely try to cut him off from the south, at least the light would be brighter and he might put some distance behind him without moving all the way down into the possibly posse-haunted bottomlands.

He was glad he was edging down easy, in such light as there was, when his heel dislodged a good-sized rock to roll down ahead of him, making a considerable clatter for some fifty yards and then . . . not one single sound for a spell, unless one counted a far-off busted-china sound, almost lost amid the soft moaning of the night wind.

Inspired to ease down more cautiously, Longarm still felt his balls pucker when he got down to where he could make out the sheer drop-off just below his exploring heels. He decided to work east a ways instead. The sneak or more with the spyglass was over that way, it was likely true, but the rising moon wouldn't light up any other route for him this side of midnight, and if there was one thing a man needed, clinging like an infernal fly to the side of a bald granite dome, a little light on the subject had to be it!

He'd eased maybe a quarter mile along the same contour line when he found himself aboard a more level stretch, almost a natural pathway spiraling downward, which was the way he'd wanted to go to begin with. As he eased along the ledge, not at all pleased by the way it sloped sort of sickeningly to his right, away from the mountain toward pitch blackness below, he perforce moved slowly enough to ponder what he meant to do once he got down off this particular chunk of moon-silvered granite. For openers, it might be best to stay down between the big bumps of bare rock. The folk after him could be most anywhere down there in the inky black ravines carved every which way through the massif. But if he couldn't see them they couldn't see him, and he had a few small advantages, aside from his desperate need to get out of this dumb fix alive.

Having nothing nor nobody to worry about but himself, Longarm knew he'd hardly need to think twice if he bumped noses with anyone or anything in the dark. Knowing it couldn't be on his side, he was safe to shoot first and ask questions later, while even mean-hearted killers might hesitate to fire blind at a careless footstep.

He assumed, from the way they'd been cutting him off all that long day he'd just survived, that most if not all of 'em were still mounted. That gave them the advantage of speed, it was true, but now that nobody with a lick of sense could consider loping or, hell, even riding a pony through such treacherous country in the dark, he had such edge as there might be. He didn't have to worry about riding off a cliff and, better yet, he didn't have to drag a possibly noisy pony along after him. He was free to move over steeper slopes as well as through thicker timber without making near the noise a pony would just have to.

As his foot dislodged another loose pebble he froze against the high side until he heard water splash, somewhere farther down than he was about to dive on a hot day when he could see where he was going. He shrugged and muttered, ''Swell, there's water running alongside us now. Let's worry about getting shot before we worry about dying of thirst.''

It was easy enough to worry about both, of course, as he

kept easing down the treacherous ledge. For now that he'd spent more than a day among the granite mazes of the Clearwater country, he could see all too well why Indian and mountain man alike had left this good-sized stretch of real estate to the lonesome winds. It didn't look like a desert, but it was. He hadn't seen so much as one deer turd all day and, inspired by hunger, he'd been keeping an eye out for anything a Digger Indian or, hell, a ground squirrel might want to nibble. But unlike the more fertile mountains he and little Ingrid Anderson had enjoyed such a pleasant few days and nights among, the Clearwaters had nothing but sort of dramatic scenery to offer. Nothing much could eat summer snow or bare granite. Down below where almost sterile granite grit afforded root holds for those few plant species thrifty enough to sprout on slag heaps, the country provided about as much forage as a city dump gone to weeds. Stock that could get by on coarse grass and maybe tastier weeds might make it, given extra oats or cracked corn now and again. But camas bulbs, wild onion and even service berries needed richer soil than he'd seen so far. He could only hope things got better as one worked farther into the Clearwaters. He was hungry enough right now to settle for bitterroot, and the mountains named for the same would have no doubt been dubbed the Sweetroots if even the squaws of the first mountain men had ever figured a way to make the damned stringy roots taste halfway decent, even with their bitter red rinds peeled off.

Thinking about eating bitterroot and ground-squirrel stew made him think about much nicer nights he'd spent over on the Blackfoot Agency to the northeast. As the treacherous trail led him down into ever deeper darkness, below the angle the pallid moon's rays now reached, he reflected that, hell, he'd spent nicer nights than this in Mexican jails. For even when they didn't feed you, you still got to hunker down in a corner and just feel miserable without having to worry about one false step hurling you over a damned old cliff.

He decided he might be thinking so gloomy because he'd made his legs feel a mite wobbly, edging down so far with every muscle tensed. So he put his back to the safe side, slid down the smooth granite on his rump, and just let his fool boot heels hang out over nothing as he willed his long legs to go limp.

They didn't want to, even when he assured them there was just no way their feet or even their boots were likely to drop off into the blackness below. He raised his knees to brace his heels on the solid albeit outward-sloping rock. It felt a mite safer. His damned legs still felt shaky and he knew the left one was fixing to cramp if he couldn't get it to relax. When it refused to, all the way, he swore and decided, "Well, if you boys won't take a nice lie-down when it's offered, you may as well be toting me somewhere."

He drew his feet in all the way and started to rise. Then he heard someone else scraping steel on rock and froze in his crouching position, straining to locate the source of the ominous but mighty odd sound. Then, striding upslope as if she owned the damned mountain, and leading her mount by the reins as if the narrow treacherous trail was ten feet wide, came a tall willowy gal in a ten-gallon hat and fringed riding skirts to bump smack into Longarm even as he warned her to freeze.

Then he, she, and even her infernal pony were all tangled up together and he knew, sickly, that no matter what he told her to do now, they were going over the edge together, whether she did it or not and, sure enough, they did, with her screaming, the pony screaming, and Longarm just having time to mutter, "Aw, shit," before they hit bottom.

Chapter 11

Ferocious Fran Ferris hadn't been heading up the mountain on her own, of course. She wouldn't have been leading the boys at all if she hadn't been up that trail to the top in her tomboy days and, hell, *ridden* her pony up it in daylight.

The four posse members following her up after Longarm hadn't shared Ferocious Fran's casual attitude toward heights. So it took them a few moments to work up to where she'd gone over, pony and all. When they lit the bull's-eye oil lamp one rider had brought along, they could read some of Longarm's sign as well. A man trying not to follow a lady and her horse over a cliff leaves heel marks indeed on light gray rock.

One of them gulped, edged as close as he dared to the drop-off and stared morosely down, saying, "Hand me that lamp, will you? I can't see shit down yonder."

The one with the bull's-eye hung on to it, but moved on hands and knees to shine the yellow beam downward. Then they both gasped and announced, collectively, "Nobody could have lived through that!"

For as the beam swept back and forth across the inky surface of the mountain tarn a good six or seven stories below, it picked up first the floating hat of Ferocious Fran and then the soggy form of her gray gelding, bobbing mostly under the surface on its side.

The one who had no control over the beam asked,

"Sweep to the sides and see if you can pick out that big bastard who swept our poor Fran to her doom."

The one with the bull's-eye did so, sweeping everywhere he could reach from up there as he muttered, "They must not have come back up yet. They might not at all, cold as that water has to be down there." Then he picked out the stretch of white water running out and down to the north, to decide with a sigh of relief, "There you go. The current's swift and the draft is shallow enough to carry human carcasses on down the valley. The pony ain't going nowhere, though. From the way it's just bobbing there I'd say the stirrup on the down side must be hung up on something. Waterlogged tree branch or whatever."

As the ten-gallon hat floated closer to the outlet of the tarn he followed it with the beam, adding, "There you go. We're going to find poor Fran's sweet cadaver, if we ever find it at all, somewhere downstream between here and the county seat, or maybe Lewiston."

"What about that other bastard the sheriff sent us after?" asked a third member of the party.

He was answered with multiple snorts and Deputy Fran's second in command explaining, "We'll find his stiff somewhere near poor Fran's, if we ever find either. What say we get down off this depressing hill now, damn it?"

A few minutes later they'd done so. Down below, in the darkness, Longarm removed his palm from the wet lips of Ferocious Fran, saying, "You can breathe easier now. But if you scream I'll have to knock you cold. I mean that, serious."

She mentioned his mother in a most unladylike way, albeit not loudly enough to justify his striking a female of the species. They both lay half awash on the sandy edge of the cold tarn, screened from above by the overhang a million years of little lapping waves had nibbled from the base of the cliff. When he saw she wasn't up to open defiance, having lost her gun as well as her hat somewhere out in all that water, Longarm hauled her all the way out on such dry land as there was under the overhang. He said, "This wouldn't be a bad rain shelter, if it was raining and we weren't already soaked to the bone. I reckon the first thing we ought to study on is warming up a mite."

She sneered, "Don't make up excuses, you brute. I know you mean to rape me. But sweet talk won't get you one willing wiggle out of me!"

He sat up and fumbled in his jacket pockets for those waterproof matches he hoped he still had on him, asking her morosely, "Why should I do you any favors, you murderous bitch? I'll allow you ain't built bad, from what I've been forced to feel of you so far, if you'll allow me to observe that a crook who hides behind a badge would lick puke off a cowpat raw."

She patted her empty holster in vain, sniffed, and said, "You're hardly one to talk, after bushwhacking a U.S. deputy and trying to tell folk you were him, federal badge and all!"

He couldn't come up with those damned matches or, come to study on it, a sensible answer to her grotesque accusation. He scowled her way in the darkness, unable to read her expression at all, as he growled, "Aw, hell, girl, you're not going to try and feed me that toad squat about mistaking me for an outlaw, are you? Even los rurales have always had the fortitude to simply hate my guts fair and square. They translate my nickname as *Brazo Largo*, it's true, but they never make up any other bull about me."

She must have savvied at least some Spanish. For she dripped pure venom as she told him, "You're really something else. I just told you we knew you'd gunned the real Longarm and tried to pass yourself off as him for some fool reason."

Then, as if despite herself, she asked him in a less venomous tone, "By the way, seeing you no doubt intend

161

to murder me after you get through toying with me, would you mind at least satisfying my curiosity about that?''

He shook his head in a vain attempt to clear it, then muttered, ''That fall must have shook us both up more than I figured.'' Then he asked her what in thunder they were talking about, adding, ''Whether you want to believe me or not, it just so happens I am the one and original U.S. Deputy Custis Long, sometimes known as Longarm, and what else could you be curious about, Ferocious Fran?''

She said, less certainly, ''Why you keep trying to pass yourself off as Longarm after murdering him just after he left Denver, of course. I mean, anyone can see why a member of that buckskin pony gang would want to bushwhack any lawman out to catch 'em. But what possible reason could you have for pretending to be Longarm after you back-shot him? Wouldn't it have been a heap smarter to just light out for parts unknown afore anyone else knew he was dead? Why on earth did you head up this way, knowing Longarm's boss, Marshal Vail, had wired us Longarm was on his way?''

The man she was confusing so with her wild as well as premature account of his demise said, ''You just answered your own fool question. If I was really in cahoots with an outlaw gang originating in these parts, and I even suspected Billy Vail knew it, I'd be closer to Indiana than Idaho right now! Who in blue blazes ever told you I was my own damned killer, and where am I supposed to be buried right now if I ain't me?''

Then he laughed despite himself and added, ''You know, that even sounds confusing to me and I know what I just said!''

As if somewhat comforted, or confused, by his good-natured self-mockery, the lawlady answered, cautiously, ''Marshal Vail never gave us all the details when he wired us that third time, warning us you, I mean Longarm, had been found dead by the railroad tracks just outside of

Gooding, and that shortly afterwards a gent claiming to be Longarm and packing his badge and I.D. only wearing blue denims and riding a buckskin cayuse, like the rest of his gang—''

"I got it," Longarm cut in. "Naturally you double-checked with old Chuck Wagner, down Gooding way?"

When she asked who he might be talking about he sighed and told her, "I can see you never, if nobody up here knows Chuck Wagner's the marshal of Gooding. Before you say something dumb about how slick I might have fooled him with a purloined badge, consider how both he and the Union Pacific Railroad would know how many dead deputies, if any, lay alongside the tracks just out of town."

She didn't answer. Some folk were like that when they suspected they might have been dumb and wanted to study on that. So he said, "Never mind where the body of Custis Long might be right now. You said Billy Vail wired you twice, before somebody pretending to be him got so cute? What did his two sensible wires have to say?"

She clenched her teeth to keep them from chattering and told him, "I never read them, myself, I'm only a deputy, and a mighty cold one at that. Are you sure you don't have any matches?"

He did, as a matter of fact. For after some exploration in the dark he'd found the little vial of waxed matches in a shirt pocket he hadn't thought of at first. But instead of confessing to that he just put an arm around her quivering shoulders and hauled her in closer, soothing, "There's no wood to burn here, anyways. You must have some notion what those real wires had to say about me if you knew the fake one was meant to get me killed as a lawman's killer."

She snuggled closer, even as she warned him, "Don't get ideas. I don't know whether to believe you or not, yet. As I understand it from just hearing senior deputies talking about it, Marshal Vail wired some time back that we could expect his top deputy, Longarm, and that he hoped we'd work with him on the matter of the Double Tipi brand.''

''Would you have?'' he asked, holding her a mite tighter because she was still shivering like jelly in a dining car.

She told him, ''Sure we would have, had there been all that much to work on. The sheriff naturally wired back he thought the Justice Department was barking up the wrong tree. We read newspapers up this way, you know, and poor old Gaston Arquette never had more than a dozen ponies for sale at any given time.''

Longarm cocked a thoughtful eyebrow and said softly, ''You sure talk sympathetic about the old breed, now, considering how you burned him out that time.''

She shook her damp head, protesting, ''Be fair. That wasn't my doing and you know it. Or you would know it had you been there. All I done that day was serve the papers on the stubborn old cuss. He hadn't paid taxes in living memory and the county does have to draw the line somewhere, don't it?''

He smiled thinly and replied, ''Ben Franklin warned us about death and taxes, but where does it say setting fire to horse barns is due process of law?''

She sort of sobbed, ''I never even told the boys to use force on the old hermit. It was Skinny Jim who thought he saw something moving to flank us from cover and threw his lantern at the barn. We tried to get the stock out. But you know how horses are around a barn fire.''

Longarm sighed and said, ''I do indeed. But Arquette and most of his stock survived, no doubt a mite more bitter and reclusive than before and, all told, he'd have only had to sell a dozen or so matching buckskins to account for a heap of reports regarding outlaws aboard the same. What did Billy Vail's second wire say?''

She told him, ''Just asking where on earth you might be and what might be keeping you. Weren't you supposed to report back by wire, yourself, once you got to Orofino?''

He nodded and said, ''I chose to get there slower but surer after it occurred to me someone was out to stop me. When I threw them off my trail they tried to skin my cat another way, by getting you part-time peace officers to do the job for 'em, if I can believe one word you've told me so far.''

She started to pull away, felt how cold that felt on the parts of her he'd managed to warm a mite, and settled for just trying to sound cold as she protested, ''You're hardly the one to call anyone else a liar! I can prove who I am, in front of witnesses, while all you have to offer is your word and a tin badge you could have stole most anywhere!''

He said, ''Right. We were talking about old Arquette and his line of buckskin cayuse ponies.''

To which she replied, sort of snippy, ''You mean you were. Nobody around here ever said all the Double Tipi stock was buckskin. As a matter of fact old Gus bred good cow ponies, not show horses. You'll find his Double Tipi brand all over the county, on horses of just about any color. Some were buckskins, some paints, while most, of course, were just plain bays, like most horses of any breed.''

Longarm was starting to shiver himself, and while he knew and suspected she knew he knew a swell way to get warm for a few minutes, the night was young, it was sure to get even colder, and he just hated to have to appear in court against a female suspect he'd gone all the way with. So he told her, ''Well, we still got a lot to talk about. But we can talk as good walking as sitting here shivering. So you'd know better than me where your boys are likely to be camping out here among these hills tonight, right?''

She had to study on that. He said, ''Have it your own way. I can likely spy a night fire from miles away on my own and you can just sit here and nurse your goosebumps if that's your pleasure.''

As he let go of her and got to his feet she sprang to her

165

own, saying, "You can't leave me here to catch my death. You have to take me with you if you expect the boys to let you live after the way they saw you kill me earlier!"

He chuckled fondly down at her and pointed out, "They saw you kill me at the same time. So there's no reason for anyone in your posse to be on guard. They'll just be waiting for morning to show 'em all the way back to town. Lord willing and the creeks don't rise, I mean to get there first."

The adventuress known as Red Robin got to knock off around midnight, except on Saturdays or when the herds were in town. But she naturally felt the need of a nightcap or more and so, this night striking her more morose than some, she didn't totter out the back door until well after the clock had struck one lonesome time. She might have screamed more than once if Longarm hadn't clapped a palm over her painted lips and gently hissed, "Hush up and listen tight, old pal. I've just loped twenty miles or more aboard a lawman's purloined pony and I don't doubt him and his pals are mighty vexed with me right now. Could you see your way clear to hide me out a spell, anyways?"

He let go of her face. She blurted, "Oh, my God! Oh, my darling! If you're a ghost don't tell me 'til you've screwed me silly!"

Then she felt his damp duds through her red velveteen and added, "Lord have mercy, you really do feel cold as graveyard clay, but I meant what I just said, you good-looking spook!"

He chuckled down at her and assured her, "I ain't quite dead. I just ain't dried out total yet. You should have heard my socks squishing in my boots when I snuck my wet behind aboard that pony, four or five hours ago at even higher and colder elevation. Even riding foolish in the dark, downhill, I can't be more than half an hour ahead of a whole infernal posse, so unless you aim to turn me in . . ."

She told him not to talk so dirty with his duds on and hauled him down the alley, through a backyard, and up some back stairs to the quarters she'd hired private, bath and no peeking, from an old lady who worked at the county courthouse and turned in early as her chickens out back.

By the time she had Longarm upstairs with the hot water tap running him a tub of soak and some kindling lit in her bitty kitchen range under the coffeepot, Red Robin knew almost as much as Longarm about his recent misadventures. He'd seen no reason to tell her about any other gals he might or might not have kissed since last he'd let her coffee-and-cake him. But, being a woman, Red Robin naturally wanted to know more about Ferocious Fran as soon as he mentioned sitting her down in some ferns and scampering ahead to fork himself aboard a posse member's pony before she'd grasped his full intent. Red Robin seemed relieved when he assured her he hadn't even kissed Ferocious Fran, but said, "I'll believe you when I get you thawed out and in bed with me, you horny rascal. I've seen that deputy gal they call Ferocious Fran. She ain't bad if a man can abide less meat over the bones than less tomboy gals, like me, have to offer."

He knew exactly what Red Robin had to offer, and the memory had inspired an embarrassing erection by the time he could get out of his cold clammy duds and into the warm bath. As he sank his privates out of sight, if not out of mind, he sort of hoped Red Robin hadn't noticed. For he didn't want to insult such a gracious hostess, but, if the truth were to be told, he needed something to eat a heap more than he needed to get laid.

But, as he might have expected, Red Robin proved herself able as ever to anticipate his every desire. For when she came into the bath from her next-door kitchen

167

with a tray of warm refreshments, he couldn't help noticing she'd taken off every stitch. He gulped, grinned, and asked, ''When did you start shaving yourself so neat, where most folk should hardly notice?''

She placed the tray on the seat of the nearby commode as she explained, ''The last time I had my hair touched up. The hair on my head, I mean. I like being a redhead. But it's distracting to notice I ain't at the most awkward times.'' Then she poured him a mug of coffee, handed him a salami and cheese on rye sandwich as well, and calmly proceeded to climb into the tub with him, her heavenly rear view facing the taps as she settled down face to face with her bare heels up on the rim of the tub to either side of him. He bit into his sandwich with a grin, saying, ''This sure hits the spot, old pal, and as soon as I can get my insides just a mite more filled with stuffing, I'll be proud to see if I can stuff your own sweet innards, as awkward as this position seems to be.''

Then he almost spilled hot coffee over both of them as he felt the sneaky pseudo-redhead's bold privates swallow his soapy shaft as if she'd known all along where to find it.

He laughed and pleaded, ''For God's sake let me finish this fool sandwich, at least!'' But she just leaned back, propped her bare elbows over that edge of the tub, and proceeded to wring him out like a dishrag with the wild gyrations of her skillfully contracted little love-maw.

He'd once told her that if only she could play a piano as delightfully as she could screw they'd have her playing command performances at the White House for President Hayes and Lemonade Lucy. But she'd gotten sore at him that time, since she took her piano playing more serious than anyone else could manage, and so this time he just went on eating and sipping coffee as she plunged her eager hips up and down like she was doing her laundry as well as him.

They wound up in her bed soon enough. For Red Robin was an old-fashioned girl at heart, when it came to old-fashioned down-home coming. The only problem Longarm ever had with her, as he feared some others had had in the past, was that Red Robin seemed to feel that if coming once felt grand, coming a dozen times in a row would feel even grander. Knowing this, he'd learned to pace himself aboard the pleasingly plump spitfire. It was just about impossible to go all the way soft in anything that hot and tight, as he'd proven in past experiments, and she didn't seem to mind if he just sort of posted in her love saddle for a pleasant chat, once he'd come in her more seriously a few times.

So as they fornicated, fed their faces, and kept themselves awake enough to do both with her swell coffee, Longarm got down to the more important if less pleasant reasons he'd had for looking her up so late and sneaky. He told her, ''I don't know whether I had that Ferocious Fran Ferris convinced or not when I double-dealt her, as gentle as I knew how, and rode for you and your help, honey.''

She said she'd help him all she could, even French, if it was really starting to wilt. He kissed her soothingly, moved it in her just enough to assure her he still liked her, but said, ''No bull, we really have to get a few local facts nailed down better. Do you know the local folk well enough to get them to believe you, should you assure the damn-fool sheriff I'm me and not my own murderer?''

She giggled and told him, ''You're lively enough in bed for a back-shot lawman. I know the sheriff and lots of his boys personal, albeit not as biblical as this. I've only been in town six weeks or so. My landlady works for the county as well, like I told you. She was the one as told me you'd been back-shot, down near Gooding. Wait 'til I introduce you to her in the flesh, poor baby!''

He shook his head and said, ''Hold on. That takes us into deeper murk. Assuming I can convince the local law I ain't a desperate outlaw to be shot on sight, how are they supposed to convince me *they're* on the up-and-up? We ain't far from where another out-of-the-way sheriff called Henry Plummer deputized a whole posse of crooks to rob stagecoaches with monotonous regularity, you know.''

She moved his roving hand back where she liked it best as she told him quite calmly, considering, ''I played piano over in Bannock, Montana Territory, a while back. They were still talking about that mean old Sheriff Plummer and the way he chalk-marked coaches packing gold shipments so his deputized road agents would know which ones to rob. Only nothing like that's been going on here in Clearwater County, Custis.''

He suggested, ''Nothing that raw, you mean. Henry Plummer was as stupid as he was two-faced. They caught him fronting for an outlaw gang as an honest businessman in Virginia City. So he lit out for Lewiston and masterminded stickups until they caught on to him there. You'd have thought he'd have seen what he'd been doing wrong by then, but as we all know he got his fool self elected sheriff in the Montana gold fields at a time the big war was raging back East and good help was hard to come by out here.''

''Why was it dumb of an outlaw to get himself a real badge to hide behind?'' she asked with a curious bump and grind.

He replied with a thrust in kind, ''It wasn't just being a crooked sheriff that got him strung up by the vigilantes in the end. It was pulling stickups so close to where he was supposed to be working that made folk wonder what their sheriff could be doing while their gold shipments were being robbed. He never learned to change the pattern as he convinced himself he was masterminding clever crimes. Any crooked lawman with a lick of sense would make sure nothing sneaky happened anywhere he had jurisdiction to make the arrest. It's letting other crooks get away with it

170

that gets folk to pondering the mysterious ways of their own elected peace officers.''

Red Robin replied, ''Let me get on top again if you feel more ponderous than passionate right now. The law here in Orofino can't be all that crooked. I'd have heard about it if anyone had been robbed here at all recent.''

As he rolled off and stretched lazily on his back Red Robin forked a plump creamy thigh across him, took his semi-sated shaft in hand to guide it where she wanted it, and settled down atop him with a contented sigh, adding, ''Ooh, I really admire a deep thinker. But can we forget about other badge toters right now, darling? They can't get at you here, and you don't have to get at them, either. The last deputy who behaved at all improper was run out of town at least a year ago, see?''

He frowned up at her to say, ''Hold on, honey. That's mighty interesting timing. You're moving your ass nice as well. What can you tell me about a local lawman said to be a crook, starting with his name, if you know it.''

She began to move faster, pouting some as she replied, ''Damn it, Custis. I told you I've only been in town a few weeks. I never saw the son of a bitch. They say he was trying to shake down the whores in town for money and other favors when the sheriff found out about it and ran him out of town. The fool should have known the girls only pay off the head lawman with the understanding nobody else will bother 'em as long as they behave half-way decent. I think they said they called him Skinny Jim. Skinny Jim Green, that was it.'' Then she giggled with delight and added, ''Oh, Custis! Whatever has gotten into me?'' as he rolled her on her back, hooked an elbow under each of her plump knees, and proceeded to reward her for being such a responsible citizen. It was only later, as they were sharing a postcoital cuddle and cheroot that he felt obliged to explain, ''A young outlaw I last met up with in the Denver Morgue was going by the name of Jim Green

171

just before he was identified as one Jimmy Hayward. He might have struck some as skinny enough to be dubbed Skinny Jim. More importantly, he was passing himself off as a stock dealer down Denver way, and another lady just put the young rascal nobody's ever accused of being honest in close proximity to old Gaston Arquette and his well-known remuda of cayuse ponies!''

He patted her bare shoulder, hugged her closer, and added, ''Yep. Thanks to you things are commencing to fall into place at last.''

So she sort of sobbed as she clutched at him to demand, ''Does that mean you'll be running out on me in the cold gray dawn again, you cruel and uncaring thing?''

To which he felt safe to reply, soothing, ''Hell, girl, it's going to take me at least a few days up here, poring through the county files, before I'll know for sure whether you just put me on the right track at last, or led me even further astray. I mean as far as hunting outlaw goes. I'm always ready to go anywhere else with anyone pretty as you, Red Robin!''

Chapter 12

In point of fact it only took Longarm one morning at the county hall of records and a day and a half in the saddle, canvassing local folk who'd known either Gaston Arquette or Skinny Jim, before he and Red Robin had to part once again, saddle-sore enough, for now.

He got back to Denver a few days after the long night letter he'd wired his home office. So Billy Vail had grown as impatient as a kid the night before Christmas by the time Longarm wandered in one morning, wearing his dark tweed suit and shoestring tie again and, just as naturally, almost an hour late.

Henry, their prissy clerk, had been doing a heap of the paperwork in the past few days. So he followed Longarm into the inner sanctum, packing a manila folder of notes.

Billy Vail had thumbtacked a big survey map to his oak-paneled wall. As Longarm blinked in surprise and turned sideways to Vail's desk to admire it, their pudgy boss rose to sort of war dance around one end of the desk, demanding, "Where in the hell have you been all this time? Anyone can see the pattern, once you make a red circle everywhere that gang had pulled a stickup! The closest they've ever hit near Denver was Golden to the west and Loveland to the north. Yet anyone can see, once he studies on it, that downtown Denver is just crawling with banks and, hell, the only U.S. Mint for a thousand miles!"

Longarm got out a smoke as he nodded soberly and said, "I know. That's why I wired you my suspicions that the ringleaders of the gang had to be headquartered somewhere here in Denver. I had to detour down the Clearwater River to Lewiston before I headed back here. They told me in Orofino the late Gaston Arquette had moved down yonder after he'd been run out of the Clearwater country."

As he lit his cheroot Billy Vail blinked and asked, "Did you say *late*?"

Longarm replied, soberly, "Losing his spread broke the ignorant old breed. He tried to start up again over in another neck of the woods. But he drank a heap heavier than he ever got around to paying taxes and they had to sell off the last of his stock to pay for his funeral."

He turned from the map to stab his cheroot at Vail and add, "That ain't as important as the two simple facts I wired you about the old man's locally famous stock. Do we have to go over it again?"

Vail shook his bullet head and replied, "Not hardly. I'll take your word that old breed never had enough stock for sale to mount much of a gang and that anyone with a running iron and a fairly steady hand could brand most any pony with most any brand."

Longarm nodded, curtly. But Henry, who'd never branded anything, waved his folder for attention and said, "I must be missing something. As per instructions I've gotten the names and addresses of all the horse traders dealing down around the Denver stockyards enough to matter. Culling out those who specialize in cow ponies of the cayuse persuasion narrows the field considerably. But there's no such brand as Double Tipi registered anywhere in Colorado, let alone this county."

Longarm and Vail exchanged weary looks. Longarm was more gentle by nature, so he softly said, "Henry, it struck me as sort of dumb to begin with to mount a whole band of bandits aboard getaway ponies sporting the mastermind's personal brand. Kate Hayward told me her kid brother dealt in horseflesh, local, when he wasn't sticking folk up. Seeing he didn't have to worry about making a real profit, swapping horses, it would have been easy for him to amass them a remuda of buckskin cayuse or part-cayuse ponies, from one cowhand here and another dealer there, in no time at all. But, not wanting us to pursue that line of questioning, down around the yards, they rebranded said ponies to make everyone think they'd been begged, borrowed or stolen off a better known cayuse breeder. Jimmy Hayward, whether he was the original mastermind or not, had been a part-time lawman and full-time sneak up in the Clearwater country, under his alias, Jim Green, long enough to learn how far and wide old Gaston Arquette's cayuse ponies were known.''

Henry nodded, understandingly, and said, "I got the part about you being led on such a wild-goose chase to Idaho Territory when all the time the mastermind was no doubt laying low right here in Denver!''

Longarm shot Billy Vail a thoughtful look, but it wasn't smart to say, "I told you so!" to such a growly boss. So he just said, "The crooks Denver P.D. traced to that livery and downtown boardinghouse were likely no more than new recruits. You can only board so many new faces and identical ponies in even a transient neighborhood before the copper-badge on the beat gets to noticing. So let's get to the mailing addresses of some more settled down cusses in the horse trading business, Henry.''

As the clerk moved over to Vail's desk to spread the contents of his folder flat the office door popped open, unpreceded by so much as one knock, and so Longarm and Billy Vail had both drawn and thrown down on her as Ferocious Fran Ferris, of all people, sashayed in bold as brass to announce, "They told me I'd find me Marshal Vail back here and— Oh, howdy, Deputy Long. I was hoping you'd be here.''

Longarm put his .44-40 away, introducing the pretty but sort of buckskin female deputy to both Vail and Henry. Vail said he'd put his own gun away if the young lady would only explain why she'd busted into his private office armed and rude.

Longarm explained everyone he'd met up Idaho way had been a mite less citified than the fashionable set of Denver, and Ferocious Fran told Vail, "A lot this deputy of yours knows about manners. First he damn near drowned me in snow melt, then he shoved me on my rump and stole a pony off one of my boys, and then he lit out on us without saying word-one about them sneaky outlaws who caused us all so much trouble!"

Vail grinned at the picture, despite himself. Then he remembered his manners and told her in a more courtly tone, "I was in the process of trying to herd him to the infernal point when you barged in, just now, Miss Ferocious. Why don't you set yourself down in yonder easy chair and listen in, if you like. We can't let you tag along, of course, but—"

"We may as well, boss," Longarm cut in. "She's a hell of a tracker, as I can assure you from personal experience, and better yet, she knows Jimmy Hayward on sight. He used to ride with her as Skinny Jim Green."

Ferocious Fran nodded eagerly, but Vail growled, "Hold on, now, dang it. I'll take your word on how tough Miss Ferocious may be, but why in thunder do we need anyone to I.D. the late Jimmy Hayward for us, even if we wanted to dig him up again? The cuss was identified by his sister, in the Denver Morgue, weeks ago, right?"

Longarm shook his head and answered, "Wrong. I don't know who that gal calling herself Kate Hayward might have been, but she had to be lying like a rug when she said either punk we had on ice was the one and original Jimmy Hayward, Skinny Jim Green, or whoever."

He saw he had all three of 'em staring at him sort of

slack jawed so he said, "For openers the bodies were first identified as boarders at a transient rooming house. They'd no doubt been told what names to give and Jimmy Hayward had used up Jim Green, for himself, up in Idaho Territory."

Ferocious Fran nodded grimly and said, "That's for sure. The one thing we agree on is crooks wearing badges. But are you saying the real mastermind, all this time, has been that two-faced Skinny Jim Green, Hayward, or whatever?"

Longarm nodded, flicked some ash on the rug to protect it from carpet mites and, ignoring Billy Vail's gasp of indignation, told them all, "Nobody else works half as well. They told me in his old hometown that he'd been born rotten and grown up worse. By the time they'd run him off his home range he'd gotten a mite slicker, albeit no more honest. Like Henry Plummer almost a generation earlier, he thought it might be fun to wear a badge and raise hell at the same time."

Ferocious Fran chimed in, "He refused to obey orders and, worse yet, tried to shake folk down with that junior deputy's star we were dumb enough to issue him."

Longarm nodded and pointed out, "I just said that. But each time he got caught he got slicker and changed the way he operated. He may have started out with one or two real ponies from poor old Arquette's auctioned-off remuda. At any rate he got the grand notion to razzle-dazzle us as we know in outline if not detail. We're going to want to take at least a few of 'em alive if you want every loose string tied neat in our final report, boss."

To which Vail replied in a growl indeed, "Let's not concern ourselves with pettifogging details, old son. Henry, let's have a look at them possible hideouts here in town, where they've no doubt been laughing at us all this time!"

Henry had worked out over a dozen with the local law. But Longarm glanced at the banjo clock on the wall and

177

said, "The odds are ten to one in favor of that place just over between Curtis and Champa. So why don't we check that property out before we ask down the hall for warrants to search any other?"

Vail grinned like a mean little kid, slipped an officious looking length of folded bond paper from under his coat, and handed it to his clerk, saying, "Fill in the blanks with that address, Henry."

Henry wasn't surprised to see Vail had already thought to ask his drinking buddy, Federal Judge Clayton, for a search warrant to be filled in as needed. But he did feel obliged to point out that the carriage house Miss Kate Hayward had long since vacated didn't appear on the list he'd worked out with Denver P.D.

Vail said, "Don't fret about it, Henry. I don't know where he came up with his odd notions, neither. But, no offense, he's caught more crooks than anyone else we got on the payroll."

Neither the state nor city lawmen Billy Vail had to get along with and Longarm sometimes had to work with would have ever forgiven them if they'd been left out of a case sure to make the front pages no matter how things turned out. So it was well after noon by the time everyone in the boardroom down the hall from Billy's office had more or less agreed on a plan of action. Sergeant Nolan of Denver P.D. was the one who pointed out suppertime, say just before sundown, might get them in less trouble than any other time he could come up with.

Longarm seconded his motion, and when a more impatient-looking cuss from the sheriff's department demurred, he explained, "Suppertime's best for two reasons. We don't want stray rounds hitting workers heading home before suppertime or kids playing kick-the-can out front, after supper. The second reason, of course, is that if the man of the house ain't there at suppertime he'll likely not be home at all.''

The gent from the sheriff's department grimaced and said, "I told my old woman *I'd* be on time for supper, and she's frying chicken for us this evening.''

Vail growled, "It could be worse. Fried chicken tastes better cold than reheated steak and potatoes, and you don't hear me complaining, do you?''

That drew some laughter, but not a hell of a lot, and when yet another morose individual asked how Vail knew, for certain, they'd get to make any arrests at all, Vail could only stare sort of sadly at Longarm, seated across the way next to Ferocious Fran.

Longarm nodded soberly and agreed, "That's a fair question. I have to confess I wasn't planning nothing this elaborate when I made no more than an educated guess. So what say Miss Fran and me sort of scout the suspected hideout this afternoon? She knows the suspected ringleader on sight, albeit not by his real name, while I reckon I could spot the gal pretending to be his older sister from, say, across the street.''

Some at the table seemed to feel that was a grand notion. But Vail snapped, "Don't you dare! That's an order!''

Nolan asked, "What makes you think you could get anywhere near the darling place without being spotted, if there's anyone there from the gang at all?''

It was Henry of all present, just to Vail's left, who announced, "Unless Longarm was dead wrong to begin with, the same people on file as the owners of record six months ago are still hanging on to it.''

A Denver lawman who kept abreast of their police blotter said, "Some of our boys interviewed the landlady later, about that dead man in her carriage house. She told our boys she might have heard some wicked boys setting off firecrackers, earlier. She seems just a mite dotty as well as deaf. It took her some time to grasp the notion of a dead man in her carriage house. She said she'd rented the rooms upstairs to a nice young lady with the distinct understanding no male visiting was allowed.''

Henry shuffled his papers officiously, cleared his throat, and announced, ''That would have to be old Hortence Gray. It's her son, a widower, who actually owns the property.''

Longarm feined a yawn, nudged Ferocious Fran, and murmured, ''I don't know about you, but if we don't get to raid that place before suppertime, I mean to enjoy me some free lunch and needled beer at a swell place just down the way.''

She started to object. Then she caught on to the smoke signals in his innocently staring eyes and said she was mighty famished, too, now that she studied on it. So he helped her to her feet and told Billy and the others they'd be back from the Parthenon in an hour or so. Vail growled at them to make sure they got back sooner and, as they were leaving, Vail nudged Henry and murmured, ''You go along with 'em and bring me back some boiled eggs, son.'' So Henry left his papers on the table and wordlessly excused himself from the meeting as well. Out in the marble corridor he didn't hail Longarm or the girl from Idaho as he saw them vanishing down the stairwell. Henry knew what his boss wanted. Henry was paid to know what his boss wanted. So he knew it couldn't be boiled eggs.

Outside, on the crowded streets of downtown Denver, Henry might have had more trouble spotting Longarm and the girl if he hadn't already surmised the direction they might be headed. They weren't headed for the nearby Parthenon Saloon. As the boss had guessed they might, they were striding in step toward the southeast, despite Billy Vail's orders not to.

Henry followed with a weary sigh. He knew Longarm would really be in for it if Billy Vail found out he was flat-out refusing to obey a direct order. He knew Longarm and the other deputies considered him an infernal teacher's pet and office snitch, too, even though he was simply, sob, trying to do his job. As Longarm and the roughly clad but good-looking gal swung a corner, Henry hurried to make sure he didn't lose them. Maybe, Lord willing, they were only heading off somewhere to get laid and, in that case, he wouldn't have to tattle on Longarm after all.

By the time they'd crossed 16th on foot and were striding into ever less fashionable parts of town, Longarm had brought Ferocious Fran up to date on his adventures with the mysterious Kate Hayward, cleaning the story up a mite, of course, and the female peace officer tended to go along with his reconstruction of the events that had sent him six hundred miles and change out of his way. She asked, "What do you reckon happened to the real Kate Hayward?"

He just shrugged and answered, "Quien sabe? Neither she nor their old man had been around for some time by the time I passed through. The sneaky gal who said she was Hayward's sister, and that he was dead, must have known nobody would be there. In fairness to a mighty sneaky little sass, the Kate Hayward I met up with here in Denver combed her hair and kept her nails neat. The quarters above the carriage house we're headed for had been swept and even dusted shortly before my short visit. The Hayward house up north hadn't been kept fit for pigs to snort at and the folk up yonder who'd known the no-good's older sister recalled her to me as a more stupid than really wicked slattern who lied with more vigor than skill. The one who told me she was the caring sister of a poor dead outlaw was a more skilled liar as well as a neater housekeeper. For openers she knew all the time that neither dead men at the Denver Morgue could be the real Jim Hayward. For their whole plan hinged in getting us to believe Hayward was dead. Things had gone to hell in a hack on 'em. We'd wound up with dead bodies and live ponies that could be traced back to them if they gave us time to study on things halfway calm. Worse yet, one member of the bunch we jumped out by the clay pits that fatal day had streaked straight for the gang's real head- quarters, instead of wherever they'd planned on him going on that fast and shifty footed cayuse. He showed up wounded and fixing to die, or maybe they fixed him for showing up at all by gunning him themselves. Either way, they had a heap of loose ends and possible eyewitness accounts to cover. So they sent the fake sister to lure me to that carriage house, fired a harmless shot at me in the dark to purloin the letter further, and—''

''Hold it!'' she cut in. ''How did purloined letters get into this story?'' So he took her gently by one elbow to steer her around a pile of horseshit as they crossed the next street and asked if she hadn't ever read that swell story by Poe.

She asked, ''Do you mean the one where the crook's trying to hide this letter from the law and so, knowing they'll be searching his quarters high and low he leaves it on his desk in plain sight, knowing that's the last place they'd expect to find it?''

Longarm nodded and said, ''Exactly. You heard the Denver P.D. back there say they'd checked things out where we're headed. I had the word of an outlaw's sister that he was dead. I not only vouched for that but went along with the notion the dead man found smack on the property didn't belong there, any more than his pony. I thought I was walking a lady home to her lonesome quar- ters over an empty carriage house because she'd *told* me so. It just never occurred to me she knew, she had to know, there was a dead boy and a live cayuse where she was leading me so sweet and innocent.''

''Knowing her confederates would make sure you never got a good look at the place until it was time for you to place her off the premises at the time of the killing!" marveled Ferocious Fran. "I'm beginning to see it all, now. They threw you and all the other lawmen down here off by persuading you the trail led north, up our way, where not one of the rascals had been for over a year! But then why did they try to keep you from getting to Orofino alive after all the trouble they took to send you out along that false trail, Custis?"

He said, "Oh, that's the easy one. They knew that once I got to talk to anyone halfway honest in the Clearwater country it wouldn't take me any longer than it did to see what a false trail I was on. They didn't want me meeting up with you or anyone else who knew what the real Jim Hayward really looked like, once they'd convinced my whole outfit he was dead, buried, and not half as skinny. They figured if I was gunned, up Idaho way, Billy would never rest until he tracked down my killers, up Idaho way, and since they had no intention of ever going back—"

"You're right. That part's simple," she cut in. "I'm sure glad you got away from me and the boys that time. It would have been duck soup for anyone who'd ever worked as a deputy in Clearwater County to compose such a convincingly false message to us, after you'd foiled their simpler plans for your demise. How much farther do we have to go now? I'm not used to walking this far in riding boots, damn it."

He said, "There's times for riding and there's times for walking when you pack a badge. That's how come I wear low-heeled army boots no matter how Texicans snicker at me. We want to turn left at the next corner. We ain't going direct to the so-called Gray property. You heard my boss tell us not to. But there's an old brick church across the way from the main house. I'm sure the sexton will let us up in the bellfry if we ask polite at a side door, safe from view from the house. Someone at the church may even be

able to tell us if the widower Gray and his sweet old mother have been seen around the neighborhood of late.

She chuckled and said, "I noticed when you perked up at the name on the property deed. I thought you said that other lady was a smart liar."

He shrugged and said, "It was likely your old deputy, Skinny Jim Green, who came up with imaginative names like Brown, Black, and now Gray. The gal, like I said, lied with real enthusiasm. See that alley entrance just ahead? Well, when we get there don't look in, look out. We want to get over on the far side of their block before we even slow down curious."

She didn't argue. His words made perfect sense, which was why they might have gotten them both killed as they crossed the slot between backyard fences if Henry, behind them, hadn't let out a whoop a Comanche might have taken pride in. For Henry had seen the coach-and-four pull out of the alley behind them, just as the three men and one woman seated behind the driver spotted Longarm and Ferocious Fran and reacted as one to the distressing sight.

Longarm didn't waste precious time wondering who'd just shouted his name in vain. It sounded serious. He shoved the Idaho gal on his left through a picket fence with a stiff left arm as he went for his cross-draw six-gun with his right and sort of tried to screw himself down through the sandstone walk as he spun on one boot.

He still got his hat blown off by one of the fancy dressed but fowl-mouthed cusses lobbing lead and remarks about his mother his way. Then Henry, down the other way, pegged a shot at their driver, hit one of their carriage horses in the rump instead, and at least got everyone to fall down as the team bolted across the way to just miss a big cottonwood, themselves, but ran the carriage into it in a swell kindling wood smashup.

As everyone rolled out, loaded for bear and full of fight, old Henry drew first blood by setting one of them in the dust with a round in the ass. Longarm hit the one doing most of the shooting just above the heart. Then, as what seemed to be a little old lady ran for the alley entrance with surprising speed and grace, Ferocious Fran rose like Venus from the waves, albeit in this case the remains of a rose-covered picket fence that would never be the same, to nail the dear old thing through the head and somersault her in a flurry of black taffeta to land dishrag limp in the middle of the roadway.

By this time everyone else had his hands up, and since they were bleating like sheep for mercy, Longarm called out, "Don't kill any more of 'em, honey. Our pals who missed the fun are going to want some names and addresses out of the ones left."

By this time Henry had run up the street to join them near the carriage. Longarm said, "Howdy, Henry. I hope you'll see fit, in reporting all this to the boss, that neither me nor Miss Fran were within half a block of their hideout when they chose to go for a sudden spin in the country. They must have had at least one in with the Denver P.D. if they knew we were fixing to raid 'em later this evening."

Henry said he could follow Longarm's drift, and suggested Vail was never all that unreasonable when things turned out so grand. He added, "Tracking down all the confederates I feel sure these boys will want to tell us about ought to keep you and the other deputies too busy for the marshal to fuss at, for a spell."

Ferocious Fran, who'd been examining the old dead woman with interest, came over to join them, marveling, "You know, that old lady wasn't an old lady at all. She can't be as old as the derringer she was packing, once you discount her face paint and goat-hair wig." Then she spotted the one Henry had shot in the ass and said, "Well, howdy, Skinny Jim! I was hoping we'd kilt you, too. But you can't win 'em all, I reckon."

But both Longarm and Henry brightened at her words

and Longarm told her, "Bite your tongue, honey. If we have the ringleader, alive and feeling talkative, we got this case wrapped ten times better than usual, and I mean to celebrate like hell as soon as we can get us some infernal copper badges around here to take over!"

She smiled demurely and allowed she was sort of looking forward to some hell raising herself, if only she could find some sweet local boy to show a poor old widow woman from Idaho the wicked wonders of such a big town.

So by sundown they'd escaped to let more officious and less fun-loving peace officers sweat the survivors of the shot-up gang, and while Ferocious Fran found an Italian supper at Romano's romantic as anything, it seemed to make her sleepy, for it seemed no time at all before they'd wound up in bed, enjoying all the sights the sweet country gal really wanted to see, after all was said and done.

Watch for

LONGARM AND THE REDWOOD RAIDERS

one hundred thirty-second novel
in the bold
LONGARM series
from Jove

coming in December!